DELIVER US FROM EVIL

A Hennessey and Yellich Mystery

Peter Turnbull

Severn House Large Print
London & New York

This first large print edition published 2012
in Great Britain and the USA by
SEVERN HOUSE PUBLISHERS LTD of
9-15 High Street, Sutton, Surrey, SM1 1DF.
First world regular print edition published 2010 by
Severn House Publishers Ltd., London and New York.

British Library Cataloguing in Publication Data

Turnbull, Peter, 1950-
    Deliver us from evil. -- (The Hennessey and Yellich series)
    1. Hennessey, George (Fictitious character)--Fiction.
    2. Yellich, Somerled (Fictitious character)--Fiction.
    3. Police--England--Yorkshire--Fiction. 4. Canadians--
    Crimes against--England--Yorkshire--Fiction. 5. Murder--
    Investigation--Ontario--Fiction. 6. Detective and mystery
    stories. 7. Large type books.
    I. Title II. Series
    823.9'2-dc23

ISBN-13: 978-0-7278-9894-4

Severn House Publishers support The Forest Stewardship Council
[FSC], the leading international forest certification organisation. All
our titles that are printed on Greenpeace-approved FSC-certified paper
carry the FSC logo.

ONE

Wednesday, March twenty-fifth,
08.35 hours – 14.37 hours
in which a chilled discovery is made and a murder is announced.

Tranquillity. That was the word. He thought the word to be 'tranquillity'. It was the only word to describe the panorama.

Everything seemed to him to fit perfectly. It seemed to the man that it all fitted so neatly and so beautifully together, like a high quality jigsaw puzzle or a well executed landscape painting. Everything gelled. Nothing jarred. Nothing was out of place. The overriding impression and indeed, he believed, the overall actuality was one of peace and stillness combined. It was, he pondered, quite possible to have peace without stillness and it was equally possible to have stillness

5

without a sense of peace, as in the approach of, and aftermath of, violence, but here, now, was both peace and stillness combined. Tranquillity.

The water first. The water in the canal, dull, grey, dark grey, utterly uninviting in itself, was still, a smooth, mirror-like surface, so still that it could in other circumstances be mistaken for a solid. It was not disturbed by a solitary ripple or wash, by a bird landing upon it, nor a pebble wantonly thrown. There was, observed the man, a certain depth, a certain maturity about the placidity of the canal water, in that because there had been no wind in the night, nor during the previous day, the water had fully settled over time into a great calm. So it seemed to the observer.

Then, secondly, there was the ribbon of land at either side of the canal. Again, also so still, the coal black towpath glistened with isolated frozen droplets of water amid the grit, and the close cropped vegetation at both sides of the towpath was covered with a thick layer of hoar frost. It was solid, stiff, unmoving. A very late frost for the time of year, but nonetheless it was a frost-encased landscape which, like the canal, seemed to the man to be gripped with a stillness that was greater, deeper somehow, than the state caused by a simple absence of movement. The flat fields beyond the canal, surrounding it, were similarly covered in a thick layer of frost, as were the clipped hedgerows which enclosed the fields.

And, thirdly, there was the sky. A great sheet of low, grey cloud that covered the scene from skyline to skyline to skyline through 360 degrees, and with no clear, definite boundary determining where land ceased and the sky began. That was the scene which met the man and reached his soul and it was the scene which imprinted itself indelibly upon his memory. It was also the landscape wherein the stillness was compounded by the silence. No bird sang. There was no distant lowing of cattle, and, it being the early twenty-first century, no unseen aircraft was to be heard flying overhead and there was no distant rumble of traffic. Perfect stillness, and also a silence so profound that the man believed he could verily hear it, for silence, he believed, does have a sound.

The woman also seemed, to the man, to

gel smoothly with the calm, silent, white landscape. She was still; utterly motionless, making no sound. He had first seen her from a distance of perhaps one quarter of a mile, noticing first her dark hair which stood out against the background, the remainder of her being well camouflaged by the long white coat and the white slacks beneath the coat and by the flimsy white stiletto heeled shoes she wore. Not, in the man's view, particularly sensible clothing or footwear to be walking in. In such conditions one's survival might depend upon one being conspicuous. Dark clothing in a white landscape, high visibility clothing at night, or when out on the hill, that was the rule. And kit to suit the purpose; that was also the rule. The woman increased her level of camouflage by being still, as totally devoid of any movement as her environment. The man had learned early in life that being still, just standing or sitting motionless is, in itself, a very effective form of camouflage. He had often seen how just the slightest movement can betray the presence of something, man or beast or fowl, sometimes something very large and which would otherwise have gone completely unnoticed. He later thought that, had it not been for the dark hair, distinct like a black dot on a white background, he might not have seen her until he was just a few feet distant, she being so rigidly stone-like. The woman, he noticed, sat on the coarse grass bank of the canal with the towpath between her and the water, just staring out across the flat morning landscape of the Vale of York. The man steadily approached the woman and as he did so, made the decision to contaminate the silence by deliberately treading on the grit on the towpath so as to create a little sound. Even though he was approaching from the side of the woman he felt it did not do to come upon her without advertising his presence. He was loath to pick up a stone and throw it into the water ahead of him, knowing that the splash would, in that state of natural serenity, be easily heard by the woman if she was of normal hearing, but stepping from the grass on to the towpath and thus causing the soles of his hiking boots to 'crunch-crunch-crunch' upon the loose grit was, he thought, sound sufficient and a sensitive announcement of his presence.

The woman, however, did not turn at the

sound of his footfall as he had fully expected her to, in fact she did not move at all but continued to remain sitting upright with slightly bent legs and hands resting together in front of her, staring with wide eyes across the patchwork of flat, whitened fields. As the man slowly, and with growing curiosity, approached the woman, something caused him to halt, to stop in his tracks. For a few seconds there was just him and her and the stillness and the silence. He then, with growing concern, broke the silence by saying with a slightly raised voice, to ensure that it carried the ten or fifteen feet which separated them, 'Good morning,' and the instant that he said it he realized that he was looking at the first corpse he had seen.

The man had, in recent years, often thought that it had been quite an achievement for him to have reached his mid sixties without ever having seen a dead body. He had avoided military service and had gone on to lead a pleasingly quiet life. His two older brothers had undertaken the unpleasant duty of identifying first their deceased father, and some time later, after years of pining, the corpse of their mother. So that all he had seen of his parents upon their death were highly polished pine coffins being carried into a church, then each out again before being lowered into a neatly dug hole. He was a man wholly appreciative of and grateful for his achievement, though he conceded that 'achievement' might not be the correct word. His 'good fortune' might, he thought, be better, and a more appropriate description. Not for him warfare or survival in a war zone, nor fighting for his life amid dreadful natural disasters of hurricane and flood and fire, but a quiet life, unadventurous, unimaginative, sometimes mind-numbingly routine, and now it was as if some greater power had deemed that he was not going to escape the experience that was the lot of so many millions worldwide. Here was a dead body for him to gaze upon and yet who, despite being deceased, was nonetheless wholly in keeping with her surroundings. A woman in her early middle years, who had just the slightest trace of a smile about her mouth and who also displayed a look of peace. It all seemed to gel, as he had at first thought, so utterly completely, like a jigsaw puzzle. Not a piece missing nor out of place.

The man quickly glanced at his watch: eight thirty-five hours. He did so because he thought the time of his discovery might be of some significance. He walked on with a profound sense of reverence as he passed the corpse, even though it might seem that he was leaving the seated woman to her reveries, but the onward path was known to the man as being the speediest route to the nearest public telephone.

Fifteen minutes later the man, having dialled three nines from a classic red Gilbert Scott telephone box, stepped from the box and viewed the buildings of the village of Middle Walsham which he felt very rightly enjoyed conservation area status: grey stone cottages with slate roofs, a village green, a pub with the intriguing name of the 'Shepherd's Retreat', a row of shops with convex windows made up of small, individual panes of glass. He groped into his pocket for his pipe and was standing by the telephone box contentedly drawing on his favourite dark shag mixture when the police patrol car arrived, slowing to a halt beside him. After the preliminaries the man gave the constables his name and address and told them where they could find the corpse of the middle-aged lady. He was quietly amused when overhearing one of the constables who spoke on the car radio describing him as 'seeming to be genuine'. The constables then walked from their car towards the towpath and the man hurried home. He had quite a story to tell his wife.

Reginald Webster carefully considered the body. He saw a small woman. Perhaps, he thought, about five feet tall, certainly not much taller. He saw a round and well nourished face beneath the neatly kept dark hair and a slightly opened mouth. He saw rings upon her slightly stubby looking fingers and an expensive looking gold watch on her left wrist. He noted rings on the fingers of both her hands. He glanced to his left at the police surgeon.

'Life extinct,' Dr Mann spoke softly in response to Webster's questioning glance, 'but no obvious cause of death that I can detect except that she perhaps froze to death. It is a distinct possibility. It's getting a little warmer now, the frost is beginning to thaw as you see, but during the night it was well below freezing ... well below ... a late frost, but a frost just the same. She, the deceased, has nothing but her clothing to separate her from the ground, no useful groundsheet, for example. It was a still night and so there would have been no chill factor to aggravate matters but it would have been quite cold enough, sufficiently cold to separate her body from her soul.' Dr Mann paused and glanced around at the white-coated fields, still devoid of any movement and sound. 'She appears to be insufficiently clothed for this weather and this level of exposure. We see nylons below the slacks but nylons are not thermal underwear and who here is not wearing thermals? I certainly am.' He looked at Webster and then at the two constables who had responded to the three nines call. None replied. 'You see all four of us are in thermals and speaking for myself, and myself only, it still feels damn cold.' He paused. 'Well ... the deceased might have walked here, just walking along the canal towpath, she stopped, perhaps feeling fatigued and in need of a rest, she sat and ... and that's all it would have taken, just sitting down on cold ground in sub-zero temperature wearing nothing but flimsy, fashionable clothing. Frankly, this could even be a suicide: such is not unknown.'

'Really?' Webster again glanced at the tall turbaned police surgeon.

'Oh, most certainly, yes, deliberately inducing hypothermia is a tried and tested means of suicide and has a number of advantages: it's clean, certain, doesn't involve anybody else. The pain of the cold is intense, that is the one drawback ... but only initially so ... the feeling of the cold passes as the body becomes numb and the blood is pulled from the extremities to keep the inner organs insulated, but the body doesn't recognize the brain as a vital organ and so drains blood from the head into the chest cavity. Thusly the person begins to experience light-headedness and a wholly unfounded sense of euphoria and consequently the last moments of consciousness are of emotions which are deeply happy and content. You see the good lady's mouth? That might even be a smile we see, formed as she sat here feeling deeply content and at peace with the world as her body stiffened. I can think of worse deaths.

Much, much worse, as I imagine you can.'
Again he paused. 'Well, I can do no more ...
death is hereby confirmed. She is life extinct.
I asked for the pathologist to attend before
you arrived, Mr Webster, and...' Dr Mann
fell silent as he looked along the length of the
towpath, 'I do really believe I see Dr D'Acre
coming now ... this is her, is it not?'

Webster turned and saw four figures walking as a distinct group with determination
and a sense of purpose, he thought, towards
them from the direction of the village of
Middle Walsham. Webster made out the tall,
slender figure of Dr D'Acre in the lead,
behind her was the well set figure of DCI
Hennessey, and behind him two constables
walked, one of whom carried Dr D'Acre's
black leather Gladstone bag. Four dark
figures striding strongly against a white
background beneath the low, grey cloud
cover.

It took fully a further five minutes for Dr
D'Acre's group to reach Webster and Dr
Mann, the first two constables and the
corpse. After acknowledgements, Webster
said, 'Deceased adult of the female sex, sir.
No apparent injuries. Life extinct confirmed

just now by Dr Mann. Could be misadventure, but I don't think we should be closing any doors on other possibilities, certainly not this early in the piece.'

'Quite right.' George Hennessey also considered the body and he too saw, as Webster had seen, one short, early middle-aged lady who sat as if smiling and was yet deceased. He also noticed her to be woefully ill-dressed for the weather and the remoteness. 'No handbag,' he commented, refraining from mentioning her inappropriate clothing, believing it to be too elementary and obvious a comment to pass, 'an unusual absence since her watch and jewellery have not been removed by her or by another. Did you see a handbag anywhere?'

'No, sir,' Webster spluttered.

'Strange, don't you think?'

'Very strange, sir ... confess I did not notice the absence of one but as you say, strange. What woman who dresses like this lady is dressed would not have a handbag with her? Very strange.'

'It's a suspicious death.' Dr D'Acre, who was not at all concerned by the absence of a handbag, had knelt and had been carefully examining the deceased. She leaned forward and pulled the silk scarf further away from the neck and exposed linear bruising. 'They are ligature marks,' she announced in a calm, matter-of-fact manner. 'Do you see?' She knelt closer and pulled the scarf still further from the neck. 'Very clear ... see them?'

Hennessey and Webster advanced and stood either side of Dr D'Acre and looked at the linear bruising which seemed to them to fully encompass the neck of the deceased. 'Yes,' Hennessey murmured, 'yes, I see.'

'Not misadventure at all,' Webster added.

'Could still be...' Dr D'Acre turned and smiled warmly up at him. 'The bruising may not have been fatal; it could even be a few days old and utterly unconnected with what it was that brought her to die at this lonely place. There is suspicion but all avenues still remain open.' She looked around the immediate vicinity. 'There is no sign of a struggle that I can detect, no sign of her being taken by force here. So, if the bruising is relevant, it means she was attacked in some other location and carried here in an unconscious state and left for dead, or left to die in the cold. She possibly regained conscious-ness and sat upright but was by then danger-ously hypothermic and would have rapidly succumbed to hypothermia. If I am correct, she would have survived if she had been left here on a warm summer's night ... unless, of course, unless the murderer knew what he was doing and left her out here for the frost to finish the job for him ... or for her. So ... I have seen all I need to see, little point in tak-ing any temperature either of the deceased or the ground because both will show a reading of zero.' Dr D'Acre stood. 'If you have taken all the photographs you wish to take, Chief Inspector, you can have the body removed to York District Hospital for the post-mortem.'

Hennessey turned to Webster. 'SOCO have still to arrive, sir,' Webster said, responding to Hennessey's silent question. 'No photo-graphs have been taken at all, as yet.'

'As yet,' Hennessey groaned. He turned to one of the constables and said, 'Radio in, will you, find out where SOCO is ... they're probably driving round looking for us ... damn canal isn't difficult to find.'

'Yes, sir.' The constable reached for the

radio clipped to his lapel.

'Tell them it's the long blue line on the map,' Hennessey growled with shortening patience. 'The one just to the south of York and not to be confused with the railway line.'

'Sir.'

'Well, I'll make my way back to York District and await the arrival of the deceased.' Dr D'Acre spoke calmly. 'Will you be observing for the police, Chief Inspector?'

'Probably,' Hennessey sighed, feeling acutely the embarrassment at the non-arrival of the Scene of Crime Officers without whose photographs of the corpse, said corpse cannot be moved.

'Well, the frost will preserve any evidence so the delay will not create problems, and the issue of the missing handbag...' Dr D'Acre raised an eyebrow, 'well, my penny to your pound that it is where she was strangled if the strangulation is relevant ... or ... or ... it's in there.' She nodded to the motionless ice-cold water of the canal. 'Rather you than me,' she added with a brief smile.

'We have frogmen,' Hennessey followed her gaze, 'but I know what you mean. Confess, it's times like this that I'd rather be a dog handler than a diver. If we can't find the handbag anywhere we might look ... no ... we'll have a look. We'll have to look in there but at least it's a canal, not a river, it can be closed off section by section and drained. That will make things easier. Much easier.'

'Well ... I will see you later.' Dr D'Acre picked up her bag and walked back along the towpath.

'So, who found the body?' Hennessey turned to the constables, two of whom had been at the locus when he arrived, and who now stood reverently some feet away.

'Member of the public, sir,' the constable consulted his notebook, 'one Mr Cookridge ... he lives close by. We have cordoned off the canal towpath, sir ... one tape at Middle Walsham...'

'Yes, I passed it.'

'And the other at the road about a quarter of a mile in the other direction, where the towpath can be accessed.'

'I see, well you two walk back to the village and do a careful search of the towpath, mark anything that might be suspicious, then return here.'

'Yes, sir.'

'You two do the same in the other direction, as far as the road...' Hennessey paused as one of the constables answered his radio. The constable said, 'Understood', and clicked the 'off' button. 'SOCO is on its way, sir. They did get lost, as you thought ... ten minutes they said.'

'Yes...' Hennessey growled. 'Webster.'

'Sir?'

'Go and talk to the gentleman who found the body.'

'Sir.'

From a small stand of black trees in the middle distance a lone unseen rook cawed. Webster, for one, found himself deeply grateful for the sound.

'I do the walk daily, that lovely old walk; have been doing it daily for the best part of five years now.' Charles Cookridge spoke softly and did so with what Webster felt could fairly be described as undisguised pride. 'Not bad for a sixty-six year old, five miles a day, rain or shine, leaving the house at eight a.m. fortified by a cup of tea and a bacon sandwich.'

'And him never a sporty type in his youth,' Mrs Cookridge chimed from the kitchen, inviting herself into the conversation despite being out of the line of sight. 'And I should know.'

'Childhood sweethearts, we were,' Charles Cookridge explained with a wide grin. 'We both used to truant each Wednesday afternoon, her from her school and me from mine, winter and summer, so when our classmates were heaving and grunting and exerting themselves trying to shave a second here or add an inch there, me and her were in the woods doing a bit of heaving and grunting and exerting of our own. That tended to be in the summertime though. In the winter we just went for long walks if it was dry. If it was wet or snowing we just sheltered somewhere.'

'And then only latterly,' again the chime came from the kitchen, '...when our bodies were old enough.'

Webster smiled. 'Good memories ... very good memories. You are lucky to have them.'

'Better memories than throwing a javelin half an inch further than anyone else or jumping higher or running quicker,' Charles

Cookridge's eyes gleamed. 'Sporty types can damn well keep their playing fields. They are welcome to them.'

The Cookridge's home was a small owner occupied house on an inter-war estate on the edge of the city of York. Webster found their home to have a warm and a cosy feel to it. The living room in which he and Charles Cookridge stood was pleasingly softened by books in a bookcase by the fireside, by plants in vases and by a neatness which stopped short, it seemed to Webster, of fastidiousness. One or two items had not been put away, some of the books on the shelves were on their sides rather than upright, the rug on the carpet had ridden up against the tiles of the hearth. Homely, in a word, he thought. It was made more and especially homely by a live fire in the grate burning faggots. Webster had been welcomed into the house upon production of his ID and had received an instant assurance that 'wood is all right ... can't burn coal, they get upset about coal smoke but wood is permitted. A smokeless zone means no coal fires – but wood is all right' and from the kitchen his wife had added, 'No complaints so far ... tea, sir?'

'So you do the walk daily?' Webster asked, finding himself rapidly relaxing in the Cookridge house.

'As I said...' Cookridge sank into an armchair and indicated for Webster to do the same, adding 'please' as he did so. 'Five miles from here to the road bridge over the canal and out along the towpath as far as Middle Walsham ... lovely village ... then get the bus to York and another bus out ... pensioner's bus pass you see, doesn't cost anything, not a single penny piece.'

'So I understand,' Webster replied with a smile. 'Age has its compensations.'

'Indeed it does ... so, out by eight a.m. each day ... that way I get to walk by myself, that's pleasant and much less dangerous.'

'Dangerous?'

'There's the real danger of being pushed into the canal. Not funny, especially in winter time. It has happened. Youths round here think it's funny to push people into the canal if they're vulnerable ... like elderly or a bit soft in the head ... or cyclists. Cyclists are another easy target but youths like that sleep late, real couch potatoes. So I think I am safe, and in fact I am safe, in the early mornings. Done the walk since I retired and never had a bad experience because I rise early to do it. Only taken to exercising late in life ... never really been one for it before.'

'Yes, so you said. So, you saw nothing yesterday?'

'No ... of the woman, you mean? No I didn't. She could have been there for a couple of days in this weather without being found had it not been for me. No traffic on the canal in the winter, occasional tourist narrowboat in the summer and quite a few people walk the towpath then. So she was not there yesterday, at least not at about eight thirty a.m. which is when I get to that part of the towpath. It's early on in my walk you see. The whole walk takes an hour and a half. I am one third into it when I get to where I found the lady.'

'Rum do.' Mrs Cookridge emerged calmly and confidently from the kitchen holding a tray of tea and two cups. She set the tray down on the coffee table and said, 'I'll let you do the honours, Charlie,' and ambled back into the kitchen, leaving a trail of perfume behind her.

'That's useful to know, helps a lot.'

'It does?' Charles Cookridge carefully stirred the tea in the white porcelain flower patterned teapot.

'Well, yes ... the freezing conditions and the remoteness mean that it is possible that she could have been there for a day or two, but your daily morning routine means she arrived there alive or dead, but we think alive, sometime after you did your walk yesterday. It narrows down the time frame very nicely, very nicely indeed.'

'Well yes, I see what you mean ... and I often get the impression that I am the only person to walk the towpath during this time of the year. In fact I came across my own footprints last week ... it was quite strange. Just before this cold snap the towpath was muddy in places and I walked in the mud leaving about a dozen footprints, and the following morning I did the walk as normal and there were my footprints but no other footprints or bicycle tyre tracks over them. So not one person, not one single solitary person, had walked or cycled along the towpath in the twenty-four hours since I had left my footprints in the mud.'

'That is hugely interesting. As you say, it

clearly illustrates how much traffic uses the towpath at this time of the year.'

Cookridge handed Webster a cup of tea. 'Yes it does ... not much used at all in the winter. In fact you have to live locally to even know it's there. Sugar?'

'No, thank you. Now, that point about local knowledge, that is very interesting indeed. It could be hugely significant.'

'Well, by local I mean York and the surrounding area ... but it's not a well advertised canal for tourists, in fact it isn't advertised at all. You could stumble across it if you're a stranger to the area but it's not signposted or anything and you can't see it from the road until you are going over the bridge, or you see a cyclist riding steadily over the fields and then you realize that he's cycling along the towpath.'

'I see, still very interesting though, very interesting indeed.' Webster paused. 'So you saw nothing or nobody of suspicion ... other than the deceased?'

'No, I am sorry, nothing else at all. No person, no thing ... just the lady ... dare say that is suspicious enough.'

George Hennessey sat somewhat uncomfortably on a small swivel chair beside the desk in Louise D'Acre's cramped office and, as he glanced quickly round the room, which was so small that it made him feel larger than he actually was, he noticed little alteration since his last visit. The cramped confines were made even more claustrophobic, he felt, by an absence of a source of natural light. Dr D'Acre's desk with its small, ludicrously so, he believed, working surface, the photographs on the wall of her family, Daniel, Diana and Fiona, standing with Samson, the family's magnificent black stallion. He also glanced once, very quickly, at Louise D'Acre herself, slender, short dark hair very close cropped, a soft face, yet a woman who, it seemed to Hennessey, carried authority as quietly and as naturally as she breathed and who wore no make-up at all save for a slight trace of a light shade of lipstick. He then looked at the piece of printed paper within the self-sealing cellophane sachet. 'She knew she was going to die.'

'So it seems,' Louise D'Acre replied calmly, quietly. 'The lady was leaving you a present and that showed some considerable presence of mind, if you ask me.'

'Yes, I agree ... inside her shoe you say...?'

'Yes, we were removing the clothing prior to beginning the post-mortem, standard procedure for which the police presence is not required so long as we save and secure each item and of course anything else we find.'

'Yes ... of course.'

'Eric slipped off the shoes and did so with his characteristic gentleness ... he has a sincere reverence for the dead, a real respect. Didn't pull off the shoes with a rough and ready "she's-past-caring" attitude as many pathology laboratory assistants might well have done but slipped each one off as if the lady were still with us. I mean to suggest nothing untoward, it is just that I think Eric is a particularly conscientious young man and I believe that we are lucky to have him.'

'Understood,' Hennessey smiled, 'and I assure you, I didn't suspect you meant anything else at all. I too in fact have formed the same impression of him. A very good man to have on your team.'

'Good. Well, the paper slid out from between the bottom of her nylons and her shoe, so that it was compressed by her weight as she stood and/or walked. It was neatly folded, as you see. We picked it up with tweezers and put it straight into the sachet ... that was about thirty minutes ago.' Louise D'Acre glanced at the small gold watch which hung loosely on her left wrist, 'nearer an hour in fact ... time is going quickly today.'

'OK ... an hour ago ... about.' Hennessey carefully turned the sachet over and over as he examined the paper within. 'Seems like a utility bill.'

'So we also thought. In fact that is exactly what it is although in my report I will have to write "what appears to be a utility bill". Dare say we all get enough gas or electricity bills to be able to recognize one when we see one,' she added with a smile.

Hennessey grinned. He thought Dr D'Acre to be clearly in a good mood, even that modest injection of humour in her working environment was, he thought, a little out of character for her. 'Shall we see?'

He opened the sachet and carefully extracted the paper, holding it by the edge, and gingerly unfolded it. 'Electricity bill for Unit

Five, Ryecroft Glen Road, York ... and it's two years old ... but it does give an address for us to call on. Sounds like an industrial estate though; I cannot say I am even remotely familiar with the address. It rings no bells at all.' He took his mobile phone from his jacket pocket and jabbed a pre-entered number. 'Hate these things some-times,' he said apologetically, 'but there's no denying their frequent usefulness.'

'I know exactly what you mean ... all those ruined train journeys.'

'Hennessey,' he said as his call was answer-ed. 'Is that you, Somerled? I did get the cor-rect number? Good ... listen ... take someone from the team with you plus a couple of constables, get over to Unit Five, Ryecroft Glen Road, York ... no, I haven't heard of it either. Secure the premises on the assump-tion that it is a crime scene ... it is in respect of the victim discovered this morning, the lady on the canal bank ... frozen to death. As Dr D'Acre has just said, the deceased left us a present in the form of an electricity bill for that address folded up inside her shoe ... two years old, but the address is clear ... the link is significant. She evidently wanted to tell us something. She would not have hidden it in her shoe otherwise. Doubt if we'll get any relevant prints off it ... two years old ... but I'll send it to Wetherby anyway. OK, thank you ... I'll observe the PM and then come and join you there directly afterwards.' He switched off the mobile and slid it back into his jacket pocket.

'Suggest with respect that you look at the clothing before I send it to the forensic science laboratory.' Dr D'Acre held eye contact with Hennessey.

'Oh?' Hennessey was puzzled.

'Yes, I think you'll find it interesting. They are not British.'

'No?'

'No ... North American sizes, and with both English and French labelling.'

'English *and* French?'

'Canadian,' Louise D'Acre spoke matter-of-factly. 'It's your area of expertise and I am reluctant to encroach but I am familiar with your "encroach all you like" attitude ... which I value and admire and wholly agree with.'

'Yes ... that way we don't leave any gaps.'

'No ... none at all ... anyway madam was

clothed head to foot in Canadian outer clothing, coat, shoes, blouse, slacks ... all Canadian ... her underwear was British. So, as a woman myself, and knowing how nylons and underwear wear out much more rapidly than outerwear, I would guess that she is a Canadian woman who has been fairly medium to long term resident in the UK.'

'Long enough to have had to replace her underwear but not her outer garments ... so not a visitor ... on holiday or a business trip?'

'I would think not, depending upon how much she had brought over here with her, but we could still be talking about a few months ... possibly even a couple of years. I have a coat that is ten years old ... also slacks and shoes of that selfsame vintage ... hardly worn these days I concede, and readily so, but ten years old nonetheless. At least ten years old, come to think about it.'

'Thank you, that is a useful observation.' Hennessey again looked at the utility bill. 'Dirty, grubby ... as though it has lain on a floor for a long time. You know, Yellich is going to find an empty industrial unit which has had no tenant for a quite a while but where some person, or persons, as yet unknown, forced entry and used the premises to keep this lady against her will long enough for her to realize that she was going to be murdered, but with such lax supervision that she was able to pick up this electricity bill and hide it about her person, leaving us a present, as you say.'

'You can deduce all that from a utility bill?' Louise D'Acre smiled briefly.

'Well ... I've been a copper for a long time, whether I am right or not still remains to be seen but I think it's a pretty straightforward and reasonable deduction. It's not a domestic dwelling, Unit Five, and the bill itself is grimy and two years old. The premises have not been cleaned in that time but somebody, somebody, will own the building, someone will have a record of the last tenant, so, thank you for this.'

'Very welcome. We didn't search the pockets; the people at Wetherby will do that, of course.'

'Of course.'

'So, shall we get into our party clothes?'

Hennessey stood. 'Yes. I'll see you in there.'

Some few minutes later DCI Hennessey,

having removed his outer clothing and changed into green lightweight disposable coveralls which included slippers and a comfortable to wear hat with an elastic rim, stood calmly and quietly against the wall of the pathology laboratory. Also in the room and similarly dressed were Dr Louise D'-Acre and Eric Filey, the pathology laboratory assistant. It did not surprise Hennessey to hear that Dr D'Acre had nothing but praise for Filey for he too, as he had said, had, over the years, warmed to the man, finding him not only respectful of the dead but also, unlike any of his calling Hennessey had ever met, a warm and a jovial young man. The deceased lay upon one of the four stainless steel tables in the room with a starched white towel draped stiffly over her genitalia so as to preserve her dignity, even in death. All other parts of her body were open to full view and Hennessey saw a woman in her middle years, a little short in stature but not remarkably so. Perhaps she had thought herself to have been a little overweight but again not remarkably so, especially given her years.

'We had to straighten the body, as you see,'

Dr D'Acre turned to address Hennessey, 'but that will not affect the post-mortem procedure or any findings.'

'Thank you. I understand.' Hennessey smiled briefly as he replied.

'So...' Dr D'Acre turned her attention to the deceased and, as she did so, she carefully adjusted the height of the microphone which was attached to an anglepoise arm which in turn was bolted to the ceiling. She spoke for the benefit of an audio typist who would shortly be typing the post-mortem findings. 'So, we have a deceased who is an adult of the female sex and who is in her middle years of life. At the moment the deceased has yet to be identified. She is clearly a lady of Northern European, or Caucasian, extraction. She appears to be very well nourished and is without tattoos or any other form of distinguishing marks to her anterior aspect. If you'd take the shoulders please, Eric?'

Eric Filey, short and rotund, moved quickly and efficiently from where he was standing by the bench which ran the length of the pathology laboratory to the head of the dissecting table and took hold of the shoulders of the deceased while Dr D'Acre took hold of the feet. When Dr D'Acre counted 'one-two-three', they turned the body over on to its front in what Hennessey saw to be a skilful and evidently thoroughly practised manoeuvre. 'No distinguishing marks are to be seen on the posterior aspect,' Dr D'Acre continued. 'What is noted is a reddening of the buttocks caused by lividity. As she died the blood drained according to gravity and settled on the lowest point of the body at the time of death. She died therefore in the sitting position in which she was found.'

Hennessey nodded, uncertain as to whether or not the observation was meant for his ears or for the microphone. It was, though, an important observation. The police could now eliminate the possibility that she died elsewhere and her body was relocated post-mortem.

'Back again please, Eric...' And once more the body of the deceased was turned skilfully and with minimum effort on to its back. Without being bidden Eric Filey readjusted the towel to cover the genitals of the deceased.

'Rigor was established and was subsequently broken by myself in the presence of

Mr Filey. There is no indication of tissue decay. Time of death has to be determined but will likely be within twenty-four hours of the present which is...' she glanced at the clock on the wall of the laboratory, 'Eleven twenty-seven a.m. There are ligature marks to the neck of the deceased, fully encircling it, which seem to be twinned. That is to say, two distinct lines of bruising encircle the neck ... such bruising being consistent with a rope or similar, such as a length of electricity cable being coiled twice or doubled around the neck and then tightened.' Dr D'Acre lifted the eyelids of the deceased and continued. 'Petechial haemorrhaging is noted ... small dark spots in the whites of the eyes ... which is fully consistent with death by strangulation.' Dr D'Acre then closely examined the wrists of the deceased and then the ankles. 'Both wrists and both ankles show clear signs of bruising indicating that the deceased was restrained peri-mortem.' Dr D'Acre then examined the fingernails of the deceased and then looked at Hennessey. 'Bad luck.'

'Bad luck, ma'am? In what way?'

'No defence wounds, no split fingernails

caused by fighting off her attacker, or attackers, so no useful flesh and blood samples for you ... sorry.'

'No matter,' Hennessey inclined his head to one side, 'such material would have been useful but I am confident that we'll get there without them.'

'I'm sure you will. I'll scrape anyway, of course, but I do not expect to find anything of interest. It will be a somewhat futile gesture but I'll do it.'

'Yes, ma'am.'

'There are no other injuries in evidence so let us look in the mouth. The mouth is a veritable gold mine of information. Here rigor is still established. Eric, can you please pass...' Dr D'Acre allowed her voice to trail off as Eric Filey, anticipating her request, handed her a length of stainless steel. 'Give me a place to stand and I will move the world...' she said as she accepted the lever. She worked the lever into the mouth and then determinedly prised the mouth open and so causing the jaw socket to 'give' with a loud 'crack'. 'So useful being a pathologist,' she said as she handed the lever back to Eric Filey who immediately placed it in a tray of disinfectant. 'We are the only doctors whose patients do not feel pain.'

It was a joke that Hennessey had heard her make many times before but he chuckled anyway. It was, he believed, the diplomatic thing to do, the only response to make.

'She has a reasonably good set of teeth ... some decay ... certainly western dental work but which looks a little different to British dentistry and so could be Canadian. She seemed to care for her teeth only adequately. She didn't floss, there is a build-up of plaque ... she seems to have had a sort of "five out of ten, could do better" attitude towards her teeth. You know,' Dr D'Acre straightened up, 'I once conducted a PM on a young woman in her mid twenties ... tragically young to come here ... everybody comes here before their time but mid twenties, that really is being short-changed. She was a Russian girl and I kid you not she had a perfect set of teeth, caused by the bland, sugar-free eastern European diet she had lived on, you see. I do so worry when I see my son pour sugar into his tea ... but will he be advised?'

'They won't at his age.'

'Sadly, and then it's too late once your

second teeth arrive and you have by then acquired a taste for sweet-tasting food and drink. Well, to continue,' Dr D'Acre returned her attention to the corpse, 'this lady lived in the west all her life and had a diet high in sugar content. Her teeth have been quite heavily filled. You don't yet know her name do you?'

'No, ma'am, not yet,' Hennessey glanced up at the ceiling. The filament bulbs that illuminated the room were covered by opaque Perspex sheets which efficiently screened their potentially dangerous shimmer. 'Not yet ... in point of fact there might even be a missing person's file already open awaiting to be matched to the deceased. That is something for me to check.'

'Yes, seems likely if she was local but the dentistry may well confirm her ID. Dentists have to retain their files for eleven years by legal requirement. Some retain them for longer. This lady has had dental work done within the last eleven years, though not necessarily in the United Kingdom. Once I have taken casts of the upper and lower teeth, I'll remove one and cut it in half. That will provide the age of the deceased plus or minus one year, but I can say now that she is in her mid to late forties.' She paused. 'I don't think I have to disturb the face; there is no sign of head injury, none at all.' She felt gently and painstakingly round the circumference of the deceased woman's head. 'No, no injury at all.' Dr D'Acre then ran her fingertips through the scalp hair. 'No, none, don't even have to arrange an X-ray. So ... fortunately I can leave this lady to be identified by any next of kin who might come forward. She has clear nasal passages. I'll check all other body cavities for you in case she has left you other gifts ... such is not unknown. Now, let's see what and when she ate last. The stomach and contents thereof is always another good and useful source of information.' She patted the stomach as she reached for a scalpel from the instrument trolley. 'There will be some gas but not a great deal. So, deep breath, gentlemen.' Dr D'Acre also took a deep breath. She then turned her head to one side and punctured the stomach with the scalpel. The gas within the stomach escaped with a mercifully brief 'hiss'. 'Smelled worse,' she said after exhaling and taking another breath, 'dare say we all have. I still remember the bloated floater they found in the river, pulled him from the Ouse when he was about ready to burst of his own accord. It really was so very kind of the police to bring him here when he was in that state but I cleared the lab, put all the extractor fans on full, took an almighty breath and stabbed the stomach, then ran for the door, slamming it behind me, only then did I breathe. Remember, Eric?'

'Like it was yesterday, ma'am,' Eric Filey grinned. 'Like it was yesterday.'

'Even with the extractors on it was still a good half hour before we returned. We never found out who that old boy was.' Again Dr D'Acre stood. 'They gave him a name and buried him in a shared plot but he was some-one's son once in his life, someone must have known him. His liver was completely shot to hell, little was left of his kidneys but there was no indication either way to tell us if he was pushed or fell into the river and so that was it. Death by misadventure. He was named John Brown and buried in the paupers' section of Fulford Cemetery. I think of him often for some reason. I and other pathologists take a few of our patients home with us, in our heads I mean, and in that manner that poor old boy occupies a part of my mind. So he's in Fulford Cemetery now with the contents of two other coffins for company. I will lay flowers on his grave one day soon.' Dr D'Acre turned again and examined the stomach cavity of the deceased. 'Well, she was very hungry when she died, I can tell you that, very hungry, the stomach is quite empty. She had had no food for probably forty-eight hours. She is well nourished so she ate well but not for the last two days of life. In her last two days she knew hunger.' She turned to Hennessey. 'There will ... in fact there just must be a mis per report on this lady. There must be. She is not anorexic, she enjoyed food ... she ate. She cared for her teeth if only adequately so and she was held against her will for fully two days before being strangled. Someone must have noticed her missing by now and have reported it.' Dr D'Acre turned to Eric Filey and said, 'Can we turn her again, please, Eric? Something occurs to me.' And once again, Hennessey watched as she and Eric Filey turned the deceased upon her stomach as if she was of no weight at all. Dr

45

D'Acre then took the scalpel and made two large incisions to the lower back at either side of the spine. 'Shrunk,' she said quietly.

'Shrunk?' Hennessey echoed.

'Yes ... shrunk. Her kidneys have shrunk, not by much, but still noticeably so, quite consistent with being deprived of fluid for forty-eight hours. Not a good end to a life which had probably run only about half of its expected span.'

'But she was found out of doors,' Hennessey mused aloud, 'sitting upright.'

'Yes, I think you need to talk to a forensic psychologist about that part, but I would think that the murderer or murderers probably posed her body, laying it out on the canal bank and scuttling home and waiting for it to be discovered, assuming that he, or she or they, had killed her, as I said earlier, but in fact, unknown to them, she was still alive. He or she or they simply hadn't done the job they believed that they had done. They had not belted and braced it by, for example, pulling a plastic bag over her head for just five minutes to ensure that she was life extinct. In fact she was still alive ... unconscious, but still alive. She was then conveyed to the place where she was eventually found and laid there. Possibly the cold brought her back to consciousness, it can do that, it can give a body a wake-up call, but by then she was dangerously cold and entering hypothermia ... despite being in that state she sat up feeling light-headed and euphoric and looked at the lovely white landscape under the low cloud and might even have thought she was in heaven, hence the smile which you might note has now faded as the body has warmed. The smile was frozen on her face as hypothermia took her from us. So, no food or water, and thusly was less able to withstand the cold, but she evidently had full and unrestricted access to toilet facilities ... her clothing wasn't soiled. I will trawl for poisons as a matter of course but I do not expect to find any. I'll send a blood sample to toxicology anyway. So, my findings will be that she was held against her will for forty-eight hours, deprived of food and fluid in that time but had access to toileting facili-ties, though probably not a water flush otherwise she would have drunk something. She was then strangled, removed to the place where she was found and left for dead, but briefly regained consciousness before dying of hypothermia. Murder. Without a doubt. Murder.'

Hennessey nodded his thanks, 'Appreciated, ma'am.'

Less than an hour later George Hennessey stood silently beside a sombre Somerled Yellich and an equally sombre Carmen Pharoah. 'It was', they both assured Hennessey, 'definitely the place where she was kept.'

The 'place' was a prefabricated metal building with a concrete floor, which had been stripped of all plant and machinery that it might once have contained, so all that remained were a few empty shelves, a two-year-old calendar on the wall, discarded plastic bags, a few isolated pieces of paper on the floor and a chemical toilet, without any form of enclosure, furthest from the entrance doorway, in the corner. A length of medium weight chain was attached to the wall close to the toilet. Two shorter lengths of a lighter gauge chain and four small brass padlocks lay on the floor, also close to the toilet.

'Two short lengths of lightweight chain to bind her feet and hands –' Yellich pointed them out to Hennessey, 'well, to bind her wrists and ankles, I should say.'

'Better,' Hennessey turned to Yellich and smiled – 'but I knew what you meant.'

'Yes, sir ... and a larger length of chain to stop her wandering too far about the floor or escaping. The lightweight chain is of sufficient length to allow her a little freedom of movement, I would think.'

'Yes.' Hennessey looked at the interior of the metal shed. There was, he noted, with no small amount of dismay, no source of heating nor any form of comfort. The woman had just the cold concrete floor to lie or stand or sit on. The floor area was large enough to accommodate, he guessed, perhaps five or six average size cars, and the length of chain he further guessed would have permitted her to access approximately half that area. The shed itself was one of five similar sheds, and occupied a remote location on the eastern edge of the city of York, some two or three miles from the nearest occupied dwelling, or so it appeared to Hennessey.

'All the other units are empty, sir,' Yellich spoke quietly. 'That is to say, they are not in current use. They are all solidly padlocked up. It seems to have been a small-scale industrial estate, now abandoned. This particular shed had been broken into, someone had forced entry.'

'I see...' Hennessey murmured and then said, 'It explains the electricity bill.'

'Yes, sir, she had quite a presence of mind, as you say.'

'Yes ... she was kept here for two days or at least not fed for the last two days she was here ... not allowed water either.'

'Two days?'

'Yes, so Dr D'Acre estimates by the absence of food in the stomach and the shrunken kidneys ... no food or water for forty-eight hours. She would have been very cold and much weakened by the absence of sustenance. She would not have had the strength to shout, no one would hear her if she did and who would wander up here? It is too remote to be of interest to teenage vandals, and it is the wrong time of year anyway. Vandalism tends to be a summer and autumn activity, as we know, and the criminal fraternity would know the sheds had been stripped bare, that is assuming that the others are as empty as this one.'

'We still have to check them, sir.'

'Yes, better make sure none of the others contain any bad news. Is SOCO on its way?'

'Yes, sir, hopefully they won't get lost this time,' Yellich added with a smile.

'Good. She died of exposure by the way, froze to death as we first thought.'

'I see, sir.'

'But strangled prior to that and then taken out of doors and left for dead.' Hennessey pointed to a length of electricity cable which lay snake-like on the floor. 'Have you touched that?'

'No, sir.'

'Don't. The person who kept her here didn't pick up after himself ... the chain, the padlocks, it's all here and that cable was probably used to strangle her. It's all still here. It'll be much too much to hope that the murderer left his dabs on the chain or the locks or the cable, but ask SOCO to check them anyway, and then get them off to Wetherby. The scientists might get DNA traces ... they'll certainly get hers but maybe someone else's also. Do that as soon as you can.'

'Yes, sir,' Yellich replied briskly.

'I'm going back to the station. Who's there? Do you know?'

'Webster, sir. Webster's holding the fort.'

'Webster? All right, he'll do ... I'll phone him from here on my mobile.'

Reginald Webster gently tapped on the highly polished wooden frame of the doorway to George Hennessey's office and entered. Hennessey, sitting in the chair behind his desk, looked up and smiled as Reginald Webster entered. Webster always found Hennessey's office to be much on the small side for one of Detective Chief Inspector's rank and he noticed again how spartan Hennessey kept it, with just a Police Mutual calendar on the wall as the only form of softening or decoration. A small table stood in the corner by the office window upon which sat an electric kettle, a box of fair trade teabags, powdered milk and half a dozen half pint drinking mugs. The window itself offered a view across Micklegate Bar of the walls of the city, at that moment glistening with rapidly evaporating frost.

'You were quite correct, sir.' Webster slid unbidden on to the chair which stood in front of Hennessey's desk. He handed Hennessey a manila folder. 'Seems to be the deceased, sir, one Mrs Edith Hemmings, forty-seven years, and with a home address here in York.'

'It's her,' Hennessey spoke matter-of-factly as he considered the photograph which was attached to the missing person's file. 'It's a match. "Dringhouses",' he read the address on the file, 'modest address, self-respecting people, privately owned homes but by her clothing ... you know ... I thought she'd be much more ... more...'

'Monied?' Webster suggested.

'Yes, that's the word I was looking for, more monied.' He paused. 'Well, there is an unpleasant job to be done now.'

'But the post-mortem has been done, sir.'

'Yes, and Dr D'Acre had no need to disturb the face.'

'I see ... useful.'

'Yes. Phone York District Hospital and ask them to prepare the body for viewing, then do the necessary, please. I see that it was her husband who reported her missing?'

'Yes, sir ... two days ago.'

'Next of kin. He'll be the one to take.' Hennessey handed the folder back to Webster. 'Talk to him afterwards ... see where you get but don't put him on his guard.'

'You've found her and you want me to identify the body?' Stanley Hemmings revealed himself to be a short, slightly built man with closely trimmed, slicked down hair which was parted in the centre as in the fashion of the Victorians, so Webster understood it to have been. It was certainly, he thought, an unusual hairstyle for the early twenty-first century. Most unusual indeed. Hemmings wore dark clothing as if he was prematurely in mourning, black trousers, a brown woollen pullover, black shoes, grey shirt, black tie.

'Possibly,' Webster replied. 'But yes, we need confirmation of the identity of a body which may be that of Mrs Hemmings.'

'My neighbour told me that that would be the way of it.'

'Really?' Webster stood outside the front door of the Hemmingses' house in Dringhouses and found it to be just as Hennessey had described: modest, yet self-respecting. A three bedroom semi-detached inter-war house with a small neatly kept garden to the front, on a matured estate of identical houses.

'Yes. He told me that if two officers call, they will want information, but if one calls it is to collect you to view Edith's body, or a body which might be Edith. He said it was the first indication you'll get ... two call, the police have questions, but if one calls it's because they have found her body.'

'Or *a* body,' Webster replied. 'But yes, your neighbour is essentially correct.'

'I'll get my coat ... just a minute, please.' Hemmings turned and went back inside his house.

In the car, driving to York District Hospital, Webster broke the uncomfortable silence by saying, 'It won't be like you might have seen in the films...'

'No?' Hemmings turned to Webster.

'No, they won't pull a sheet back and reveal her head and face, it will be done quite cleverly, you'll see her through a glass window, a pane of glass, heavy velvet curtains will be pulled back and you'll see her.

She will be lying on a trolley with her head and face tightly bandaged with the sheets tucked in tightly round her body. You will see nothing else. It will look like she is floating in space, in complete blackness. If it is your lady wife, it will be the final image you will have of her. It's a better image to keep in your mind than one of her being in a metal drawer.'

'Yes, thank you. Thank you for telling me that. I appreciate it and you are right, it will be a much better last memory, because it will be her. I know it. In my bones I know it will be her.'

Later in an interview suite at Micklegate Bar Police Station and comforted with a hot mug of sweetened tea, Stanley Hemmings said, 'She was a Canadian, you know.'

'Canadian?'

'Yes,' Hemmings nodded. Webster again saw him as small, like his late wife, but now also noticed that he was barrel-chested with strong-looking arms and legs.

'Yes ... specifically Canadienne.' Hemmings saw the puzzled look cross Reginald Webster's eyes and so he spelled the word for him. 'It means, among other things, a

French Canadian female, or so she explained to me. *"Je suis Canadienne,"* she said when we first met. I remembered from school what *"Je suis"* meant, it's the sum of my French, and so she had to explain the rest. She apparently spoke French as they speak it in Quebec province, that is to say with a very distinct accent, in fact I found out that in Quebec they speak French like they speak English in Glasgow, not just a distinct accent but unique in terms of phrase and strange use of words. Just as the Scots will use "how" to mean "why", so the French Canadians have their own variation of the French language. But she and I always talked in English anyway. We had to, for heaven's sake.'

Hennessey sat silently next to Webster and opposite Hemmings in the softly decorated and carpeted orange-hued interview suite. He felt that Mr and Mrs Hemmings probably would have made an odd couple in life, more because of their personalities than anything else. Hennessey, for some reason, thought that Edith Hemmings must have been a spirited person in life, the clothes she wore, her courageous presence of mind in hiding the electricity bill in her shoe, that, he felt, showed initiative. And she had been adventurous enough to relocate from Canada. Yet here was her husband who dressed in a dull manner, and had a monotonous tone of voice ... almost whiny, Hennessey thought. Her hairstyle contrasted with his centre-parted style, attached to his skull with cream as if he was the very caricature of a Victorian railway booking clerk. The image of them as a couple didn't gel in his mind. He also found the job that Hemmings gave, 'an under manager in the biscuit factory', not the sort of job that would attract a woman of Edith Hemmings's taste in clothes, and he was a man who whined about having to take time off work while 'our Edith was missing'... again, not the sort of husband he would have thought to Edith Hemmings's taste.

'Were you long married?' Hennessey asked.

'No, sir ... just a few months.'

'Months!'

'Yes, sir, about eighteen, that's all. Just a year and a half, if that. I was a bachelor getting close to retirement and I thought, well that's me, lived alone, set to die alone, then along comes our Edith. We met in a pub in town. It was she who started to talk to me. I was just in there for a pint to get out of the house for an hour or two ... I get fed up with my own company now and again ... and it changed my life. I've never been very successful with women and I wondered what she wanted at first but she seemed properly interested in me and then one thing led to another and another and another and eventually we got married quietly at the registry office and she came and settled with me in my little house in Dringhouses. She was keen to know that I owned the house and that I wasn't renting it, she just wanted that bit of security, I assumed, and that's fair enough. So, anyway, I showed her the papers about the house, the little bit of mortgage I am still paying off ... after that she was OK about it. Quite happy. She was Mrs Hemmings. Mine ... our Edith for me to come home to.'

'I see.' Hennessey rested his elbows on his knees and clasped his meaty hands together. 'What do you know about your late wife's background?'

'Very little, tell you the truth. It might seem strange but it really was a very rapid thing we did. One day I was alone in the world ... not unhappy ... lifelong bachelor, the next married and the next a widower.'

'Was she employed, or did she have any outside interest?'

Hemmings shrugged. 'Well, she was not employed when she was my wife but before that ... well, she was working as a sort of housemaid but not a maid ... a helper ... like a companion, she and the elderly gentleman who owned the house, somewhere in the country outside York, somewhere like that ... out in the sticks. She didn't talk about it very much; frankly, to be honest, she didn't talk about her life very much at all.'

'Do you have the old boy's address?' Hennessey asked warmly.

'Yes, I have it. I can let you have it. It's at home though. But yes, I can let you have her previous address.'

'We'd like to chat to him. He might help us get to know more about your wife, nothing more than that.'

'It's more his family that is likely to help you. I think that he was a bit gone in the head and difficult to live with. I think our Edith was glad to get away from there. That was the impression I got anyway.'

'I see ... so ... can I ask you, when did you last see your wife?'

'See? Two days ago. Wednesday today, so last saw her on Sunday, so then that's three days ago. She left the house to go to the shops on Sunday evening about five p.m. We had run out of milk and so she put on her white coat and said, "I'll be back soon" ... or "I'll be ten minutes", something like that. There's a little shop just five minutes' walk away, you understand; it opens seven days a week and stays open late. It has to do that to compete with the supermarkets ... bad position for a man to be in, I always thought. I don't earn much at the biscuit factory but at least the hours are civilized.'

'Yes ... yes...' Hennessey allowed impatience to edge into his voice.

'So when she didn't come back after about an hour I went out looking for her. Who wouldn't? I went to the shop but the fella said Edith hadn't come in that evening. I said that she must have done but he said she never did. He knows our Edith, you see. So

I began to get worried because she had not taken anything with her, just about enough money in her purse to buy the pint of milk she went out for. I checked when I got back, all of her clothes were there, all of her shoes, all of her documents, even her passport and her birth certificate, her Canadian driving licence, her jewellery, it was all still there. All of it. She hadn't left me. She left the house to go to the corner shop to buy some milk for herself and her husband so that we could have a nice cup of tea on a quiet Sunday evening before we went to bed for the night and that was it.'

'I see,' Hennessey sat slowly back in his chair. 'Do you know of anyone who'd want to harm her?'

'No, sir, no one, she only knew me in York. That's all, just me. She had no friends ... no enemies but...' Hemmings voice faltered.

'But?' Hennessey pressed.

'But what?' Webster assisted Hennessey.

'But ... well, I didn't know her very long, she might have been my wife but she seemed to come from nowhere ... like she was suddenly there ... out of the blue ... but she did always seem to have a history. She gave the impression that she had left some sort of life behind her. But what that was I cannot say ... I do not know. Even in marriage she was a private person.'

'She must have told you something about herself?'

'She told me that she had grown up in Quebec and moved to Ontario when she was very young. She told me that. She never mentioned any brothers or sisters ... she said that her parents were both deceased. She did tell me that sort of little orphan Annie number but apart from that she really hardly told me anything.'

'What was your marriage like?'

'What's any marriage like?' Hemmings reacted defensively, Hennessey thought. 'We were middle-aged, we settled down ... quietly. We had an understanding, she didn't like too many demands made on her ... if you see what I mean.'

'All right, I understand, we won't go there ... unless it becomes relevant.'

'Thank you, sir, I appreciate that.' Hemmings paused and took a deep breath. He clearly had powerful lungs. 'She cooked the meals and kept the house tidy and did the laundry and I worked at the biscuit factory and earned our money. And that was our little house. Hardly glamorous, hardly the good life, but we ate, we were dry when it rained and we didn't fight. Never had fights ... that I appreciated. No fights. It was just nice to have someone to come home to after years of being alone. She even warmed my slippers by the fire for me to come home to. That was a nice touch, especially this winter just gone. I must admit things could have been more passionate but it was convenient for both of us and at our age that means a lot. It wasn't marital bliss but it was better than being alone and she, like me, was beyond the first flush of youth.'

'Understood. Did she seem worried?'

'No more than usual.'

'What does that mean?' Webster asked suddenly and perhaps a little too aggressively for Hennessey's liking.

'Well ... how can I describe this?' Hemmings sat back and glanced round the interview suite. 'It was her manner, she didn't like the summer. She was strange like that, was Edith. In the summer she had her hair cut short, really short ... didn't suit her. I think the style is called "boy cut". You know, as short as a schoolboy's hair and then when it was short she wore a long blonde wig and large spectacles but the plastic in the frames was just that – plastic, tinted plastic, not proper lenses. She had good eyesight did Edith ... big glasses, they were more like a man's frames rather than a woman's choice of frame. She would also walk round York with a small British Airways rucksack, as though she was a tourist, not a resident. That's when she did go out. Most of the time she stayed at home but I like to go out now and again. I mean it's fair enough. I'm in the factory all day so at weekends I like to roam. Why not? Go into York, drive to the coast for a few lungfuls of good sea air ... maybe find an old quiet pub for a beer or two, and our Edith, she'd drag her feet but eventually she'd agree to join me but only with the wig and dark glasses and her small British Airways knapsack that made her at least look like a tourist. When I asked her about it she just cut me short and said, "It's my image", really snappy, bite-my-head-off sort of reply, so I stopped asking but she was always clearly relieved to get back home and tear the wig off.'

'As if she was frightened of being seen?'

'Yes, but only in hindsight. Only after I'd thought about it for a while. At the time I thought it was no more than her just wanting to stay at home and not liking summer because she was a Canadian and more used to the cold, but now I understand Canada can be blisteringly hot during the summer so perhaps that was not it, perhaps that was not the reason. I just put it down to the words of my Uncle Maurice when I was a teenager. "You'll never fathom a woman, Stanley," he once said to me, God rest him, "you'll never fathom a woman", so I put it down to her being a woman and thereby a damn strange creature. I mean there seemed to be no point in going to war over the issue ... and I did appreciate a peaceful house. She was just much happier in winter. I knew her for two winters and one summer. She seemed to be more relaxed in the winter, always as though the dark nights were hiding her, and the short, grey days also. Well ... got a funeral to arrange now. I'll ask for a simple graveside service, there will only be me there, me and the priest and the pall-bearers, can't fill a church with friends and relatives I don't have so I won't try. So we'll lay her down and follow the coffin with a sod or two of soil and that'll be our Edith.'

'We'd like to take a look at your late wife's possessions,' Hennessey asked. 'I hope you won't object?'

'Of course,' Hemmings glanced up at the ceiling. 'All there is of them is just clothing and a few documents.' He paused and looked at Hennessey. 'Why? Do you think there's something there?' There was a slight note of alarm in his voice.

'We think nothing yet,' Hennessey replied quietly, attempting to calm Hemmings, 'nothing at all, but she was evidently kept against her will for two days, then she was left by the canal, as if her body was posed ... that speaks of motive and premeditation and now you indicate that she seemed to be hiding from some person or persons as yet unknown. You seem to be saying that she was a woman in fear.'

'You think so?' Hemmings looked at Hennessey with wide, appealing eyes, 'Not just abducted by some sicko?'

'We think nothing yet, as I said, Mr Hemmings. All avenues are open, all are being explored.'

The man walked purposefully up to the fountain and casually tossed a coin into the pool of water surrounding it. He then stood up and glanced around him, the solid buildings, the red double-decker buses, the black taxi cabs, the crowded street, too crowded for his taste. He was used to wide open spaces and few people. He turned back to the water. 'Well, I did it,' he said, 'I didn't do what I intended to do ... but I did something else. It seemed just as good. Just as satisfying.'

It was Wednesday, 14.07 hours.

TWO

Wednesday, March twenty-fifth,
15.43 hours – 22.30 hours
*in which more is learned of the deceased and Mr
and Mrs Yellich are at home to the gracious
reader.*

The immediate, and what was also to prove
the lasting impression for Webster and
Yellich was that the house and its owner had
both seen better days; both were elderly in
their own way and probably because of that
both seemed to the officers to be ideally suited to each other. Both, as Webster had just
that afternoon heard Mr Hemmings say to
describe his late wife, were 'beyond the first
flush of youth'. Well beyond it.

The house was called 'Lakeview', oddly,
thought Yellich, because any observation of

69

the surrounding area or a glance at the map of the district did not show the presence of any body of water in the vicinity. It was situated on the B1363 near to Sutton-on-the-Forest, could be easily seen from the road and was probably, Yellich estimated, a quarter of a mile across open fields from the tarmac. It seemed to occupy a natural hollow in the landscape which Webster thought unusual because that part of the Vale of York he understood to be particularly prone to flooding. The grounds of the house seemed to be generous with the front gate of the property being much closer to the road than the house. The frost-covered grounds, whilst vast, were also overgrown and it seemed to both officers that they needed 'rescuing' rather than 'tidying'. The traces of a landscaped garden could be clearly seen but the garden had, by the time Yellich and Webster called, largely been allowed to revert to nature. The building had been blackened by nineteenth century industrial pollution which had evidently been carried from the manufacturing areas of Leeds and Sheffield by the south-westerly winds. The house had an aged and worn look with the roofline at each side of the tall central chimney seeming to sag before being lifted up again at the gable ends. The house was of two storeys and, thought Webster, unlikely to have a cellar given the height of the water table in the area. The front door was set significantly to the right hand side of the building and enclosed in a wooden porch which, like the house itself, was decayed, with peeling paintwork and one or two broken panes of glass. The building was, he observed, potentially very interesting but had sadly been allowed to deteriorate to the point that it was, unlike the garden, clearly beyond rescue. It had been, by all appearances, crumbling for some considerable time and would continue to crumble until it was bulldozed into extinction, to be remembered only in the dim recesses of individual memories and old sepia prints which captured it in its heyday.

Yellich halted the car on crunching gravel in front of the misshapen metal gate and, without waiting to be bidden, Webster, the junior officer, left the car and walked to the gate. It was, he found, fastened to the drystone wall with only a loop of blue nylon rope which was noosed over a protruding stone in the top of the wall. He unhooked the rope which allowed the gate to swing on its hinges with a loud squeaking sound that seemed to penetrate the still silence and to do so deeply. He looked about him. The frost was obviously not giving up without a struggle and the sun had that day been unable to penetrate the grey cloud cover. The black of the house and the black of the leafless canopy of a stand of trees were the only other colours he could detect. Webster stood by the gate as Yellich drove the car slowly through the gateway. He then closed the gate and secured the loop of rope over the stone in the wall. Then there was only stillness and silence.

Webster rejoined Yellich in the car and Yellich approached the house, continuing to drive slowly, and – sensibly, thought Webster, very, very sensibly – sounded the horn as he did so. Rural dwelling people have a larger sense of personal space than the urban dwellers, so Webster had noticed and had also been advised, and do not care to be taken by surprise. A dog was heard to bark, clearly in response to the sound of the car's horn. As the car approached the house the officers saw the lean-to, which had been hidden from view by shrubbery, and which sheltered two vehicles. One, very practically, thought Yellich, was a Land Rover, the other a Wolseley saloon, white, with a red flash, of 1960s vintage. The dog, when it appeared, was a large Alsatian, alert, well groomed and clearly well nourished. It had the run of the grounds and as Yellich halted the car it put its large, very large, paws up against the window of the driver's side and barked and growled menacingly.

'Nice doggy ... good doggy,' Yellich said with a smile. Beside him Webster chuckled and said, 'After you, sarge ... you go first ... he seems to like you.'

Caution sensibly being observed, Yellich and Webster sat inside the car for, they later estimated, two or three minutes, until an elderly man appeared, exiting the ancient house via the decaying wooden porch. He stood looking suspiciously at the officers. Yellich held up his ID and wound the window down an inch and yelled, 'Police'. The elderly man nodded and called the Alsatian back to where he stood and, as it reached him, bent and ruffled its ears as Yellich heard him say, 'Good boy, good dog'.

'Police,' Yellich said again as he and Webster stepped out of the car.

'Yes ... I gathered.' The man was stooped with age and walked with the aid of a gnarled wooden stick which he gripped tightly in an equally gnarled hand. Both officers had the impression that the man had once been powerfully built and athletic. 'Can I help you?' he asked, speaking with a cultured voice of received pronunciation without any trace of a regional accent.

'We hope so, sir. Is this the house of Mr Beattie?' Yellich asked.

'It is.'

'Mr Alexander Beattie?'

'It is,' the man held eye contact with Yellich, 'I am he. Confess I have not been called Alexander for a while though, Alex is usually it. It's been Alex for a long time now ... an awful long time.'

'Yes, sir. Can we have a word with you, please?' Yellich replied with a smile. 'We just need some information; it's nothing for you to worry about.'

'I'm eighty-three,' Beattie responded with a similar smile. 'It'll have to be pretty damned serious for me to be called on by the police for something I've done amiss...' he laughed softly and warmly. 'Mind you, the company in jail would be welcome ... no ... no ... probably not, but do come in. Don't mind the dog, he's got a loud bark, but he's got failing hind legs. He can't stand for very long before his hind quarters give way ... a bit like his owner really ... it's a design fault in Alsatians, so the vet once told me. You could even probably outrun him. Well, one of you would get away anyway and his bite ain't what it used to be. None of us is getting any younger. It seems the way of it is that some of us just have to hang around the old place longer than others but nobody's clock goes backwards. Do come in.' He turned his back on the officers and walked slowly towards the house. He wore brown cavalry twill trousers, a bright yellow cardigan and black shoes. Despite being stooped with age Yellich guessed Beattie was probably still six feet tall, and that he would have cut a fine figure in his day.

Yellich and Webster followed Beattie into his house and saw that the interior was as original and as tired as the exterior. The porch gave directly on to a large kitchen with an unevenly stone-flagged floor and a large, solid table covered with a green cloth. To the left, as the officers entered, was an ancient cast iron range. The rear door of the kitchen gave way to a scullery with a door with a glass pane which looked out on to the overgrown rear garden and to the white-coated hills beyond. Beattie took a kettle and filled it from the taps of a galvanized iron sink which stood beyond and beside the range. The taps seemed to Yellich to be original and were clearly attached to lead piping which, he thought, would throw the health and safety people into apoplexy, but they had evidently done Alexander Beattie little harm and he doubted that the cup of tea they were going to be kindly offered would similarly be harmful to either him or Webster. He glanced round the kitchen and suddenly felt himself to be in a time capsule. He searched for some precise indication of the date of the building and, finding none, he settled for 'about two hundred years old, early, very early nineteenth century'. The elderly Alsatian had walked slowly to a blanket in the corner by the scullery door and had collapsed resignedly upon it, no longer being concerned by Yellich and Webster's presence.

'So how can I help you?' Beattie struck a match, held it to a ring on top of the range, and the gas of the stove ignited with a loud 'woosh' sound. He put three mugs on the table and took a bottle of milk from a bowl of water in the sink and put it beside the mugs. He then put the kettle atop the gas flames.

'It's about a lady called Edith Hemmings,' Yellich said.

'Edith Hemmings?' Beattie looked puzzled. 'Sorry ... gentlemen, oh do please take a seat by the way. Edith Hemmings ... I am sorry, I can't place that name.'

'We believe that she used to work here.'

'I have had a few helpers ... companions so-called, all employed by my son ... Edith ... but no Edith. That is an old and quite an unusual name in fact – I knew one girl of that name in my youth. I'd remember another Edith. I am sure I would.'

'A Canadian lady,' Yellich prompted.

Beattie groaned. 'Oh, her...' a note of anger crept into his voice. He leaned back against the range. 'That damned female!'

Yellich and Webster glanced at each other. Yellich said, 'I see we are in the right place.'

'Yes,' Beattie moved to his right and rested against the sink. 'If it is about her, then yes, you certainly are in the right place. Must be all of two years since she left, probably a little more. I didn't know her as "Edith" though; it was "Julia" when she was here.'

'She lived here?'

'Yes, as you see, this house is too remote for a daily help, so yes, she had a room here. All my companions did. My son appointed her, dare say he meant well. He's retired now ... and ... well, he has his family and health issues, so he planted her here to look after the old boy so he wouldn't have to worry about him, just as he planted other women here before Julia. She was a daily help ... a housekeeper ... a companion all rolled into one. Very few want to live here, and none who are prepared to do so ever remain very long. You know over the years I have come to realize that the sort of women who are pre-pared to live and work here are those who do so for the same reason that men join the French Foreign Legion. Running away, d'you see? They want a place to hide ... or a place to forget their past.'

'Interesting.'

'She was the last companion I had. Prefer it alone now anyway ... me and Ben Tinsley, we keep a watchful eye on each other. His house is that way.' He pointed to the wall behind him as the aluminium kettle began to whistle. 'We each leave a light on, a specific light in each of our houses, it's on all night. If his isn't on when I retire for the night I phone him and if he doesn't answer I will phone you good people and ask you to check on him, if you can. If you say you can't, for any reason, I check on him the next morning and he does the same for me. He's a cur-mudgeonly old billy goat ... dare say he thinks the same of me but we are useful to each other. I also move my Land Rover, take it out of the shed and leave it at the front of the house, then put it under cover again at night just to let him know I'm alive during the day. He does the same thing with his Land Rover. Haven't moved it yet so I'll do that when you've gone or he'll be phoning me. It also helps to keep the burglars away, some movement makes the house look lived in. Nothing to steal anyway.' He slowly and carefully poured a little boiling water from the kettle into a large china teapot, rinsed it out, holding it with both hands, then reached for a packet of loose tea. He put four generous teaspoons full of tea into the pot and then poured in the remainder of the steaming water from the kettle.

'Mrs Hemmings ... or Julia...'Yellich pulled the conversation back on track, 'the Canadian lady...'

'She wasn't a lady,' Beattie responded quickly and indignantly. 'And she was Canadienne,' Beattie spelled the word, 'or so she claimed. A French Canadian female, *le Canadienne yclept "Julia"*. I did believe her on that point because Mrs Beattie, by coincidence, was also Canadian. You see, in the days when all the UK seemed to be emigrating to Canada and Australia and New Zealand, she emigrated east to the UK, bless her soul, to search for her fortune. We found each other and had a long and very happy union.'

'Congratulations,'Yellich smiled.

'Yes ... I ... we were very fortunate and I am not ungrateful, not ungrateful at all. I have sat on the sidelines of some very bloody divorces in my time, and yes, we were a lucky pair. Ours was a good marriage. A very good one. I do not worry about Mrs Beattie now, she is safe. I would have worried greatly about her if I had gone before. She never did well on her own but I am a much more independent spirit than she was.' He poured the tea from the pot into the mugs and invited the officers to help themselves to milk. Both did so. 'So, the Canadienne,' Beattie sat at the table with Yellich and Webster, 'well, she came from French Canada, so she said, a small town called Montmorency which is near Quebec City. I looked it up once and it is there, right where she said it would be, on the banks of the St Lawrence, a few miles downstream from Quebec. She left the town when she was five, so she told me, and she hinted at a bit of a tough life ... poverty, orphanage ... that sort of thing. She didn't talk about her early life much but she definitely was Canadian. Having lived with one for the best part of half a century, I should know, she was the real thing, believe me. "The real deal," as my great grandson might say ... he has a strange way of talking ... children seem to these days. Sugar, gentlemen?'

'No, thanks,' Yellich said.

Webster also politely declined.

'She spent most of her life in Barrie ... so she told me.'

'Barrie?'

'Yes,' Beattie spelled the name, 'so Barrie in Canada, not Barry in South Wales. It's a town, beside a lake, if not a city, of generous size to the north of Toronto in Ontario province. Mrs Beattie actually came from Toronto and we used to visit her family for extended holidays, usually over Christmas, always damned cold it was. I would often say I would not be dreaming of a white Christmas this year, I am going to see one.' His chest heaved with suppressed laughter as he gripped his mug in large, reddened hands. 'Occasionally we'd go across in the summer but usually we visited at Christmas; my in-laws liked to have their family around them at Christmas. It was a bit of a tradition with them. Well she, the Canadienne, the one you know as Edith and I knew as Julia, knew Toronto very well, very well indeed, like she was a native of the city. She and I would talk about it, the city, and she knew the place, she knew it all right, knew little streets and bars and parks in the suburbs, but she always insisted that Barrie was her home. She might have been born in Montmorency but her roots were in Barrie. It's about an hour's drive north of Toronto which is close in Canadian terms. Very close, believe me. In fact one of my brothers-in-law used to drive two hours to work and two hours back again. He thought nothing of it, which astounded me.'

Webster groaned. 'Astounds me also, sir.'

'Yes,' Beattie glanced at him, 'hardly bears thinking about, does it? Up at six, leave for work at seven, back home again twelve hours later having driven over four hundred miles ... five days a week. He spent the weekend recovering and then was up again at six on Monday morning and off he'd go. I used to commute from Beverley to Hull – I was a buyer for a shipping line until I retired twenty years ago – and my brother-in-law once said he thought my journey to work was like a walk to the bottom of the garden and back.'

'Edith ... Julia,' Yellich appealed.

'Yes ... sorry.'

'Do you know how or why she came to be

living in the UK?'

'No, I don't, she never said why. She came to me from a fox-hunting family in East Yorkshire. It turned out that the glowing reference she came with was a piece of convincing fiction. Fellow wrote it to get rid of her. Now I know why.'

'We'll have to visit him. Can you let us have his address?'

'Yes. No problem ... I have it filed away.'

'So what did she do in this house?'

'In terms of her employment or her crimes?' Beattie raised his eyebrows.

'Both.'

'She arrived carrying just one suitcase ... and quickly settled in, seemed to be quite pleased, quite content. She seemed to have a no-one-can-get-at-me-here sort of attitude. You remember the French Foreign Legion Syndrome I mentioned? She was escaping; she was running away ... that was a strong impression I had and my old and remote house seemed to suit her purpose, admirably so.'

'Yes ... you said, it appears to be a significant observation.'

'So, she was supposed to be a daily help

and a companion, a housekeeper all rolled into one. No precise job description. She used the car to go shopping – the Wolseley, she couldn't handle the Land Rover, so she used the Wolseley. I gave her an allowance for that, to buy petrol and food for the both of us, and she was a little liberal with it, more than a little liberal if truth be told.'

'Oh?' Yellich sipped his tea.

'For example, she left at three p.m. to drive to the village to buy some food for the old boy,' Beattie tapped his chest, 'and she would return at midnight smelling of alcohol and the old boy went without his supper.'

'I see.'

'That tended only to happen latterly. She was here for about six months and she tended to stay out late drinking the food money only in the last week or two. But by the time she left my bank account had been plundered.'

'How did she manage that?'

'She had access to the cheque book for my current account. She forged my signature and bought things by mail order which she then pawned or sold for a fraction of their true value, or so my son believed when he looked into the matter. I never knew about it because she would take delivery of the parcel when it arrived. We found a lot of pawn tickets in her room and it was my son who then put two and two together.'

'Did you report that to the police?'

'Oh yes ... yes, we did straight away, of course we did, but the police said they couldn't do anything until she "surfaces", as they put it. But she had gone deep; I wasn't going to get any money back nor was I going to recover the valuables she stole from the house. She was very cavalier in her attitude. She was the "Cavalier Canadienne". She pursued her own agenda, didn't seem to take anything seriously apart from her own survival, of course ... laughing at me as she bled me dry ... she was aloof ... she was distant ... she was...'

'Cavalier,' Yellich finished the sentence. 'Yes, we get the picture. We grasp the character. "Cavalier" seems just the word, the very word.'

'But worried,' Beattie added, 'she was also worried. Exploiting me but also was always glancing over her shoulder. Sleeping, it seemed, with one eye open. There was something, some person in her life that she wasn't cavalier about. She was afraid of being seen, I mean afraid of being recognized.'

'You believe so?'

'Yes. You saw my lovely old Wolseley, 1968 model?'

'We did notice it. Nice car.'

'Yes. I like it. It's the only one in the Vale ... a classic.'

'Yes.'

'Well ... Old Ben, the grumpy old boy who looks for my light each night as I do for his, he told me a few times that he had seen a blonde woman driving the car. It transpired to be madam with a wig upon her head. That we pieced together after she had gone.'

'We?'

'My son and grandsons.'

'I see.'

'Did she leave anything behind?'

'Nothing at all of any value.'

'I have a note of the crime number the police gave me together with the address of the fox-hunting lowlife that gave her such a glowing reference that caused my son to appoint her. That's all that remained of Julia Ossetti.'

'You could take action against him, sue him, for example.'

'What with?' Beattie forced a smile. 'I have no money, hardly anything in the bank, just a small pension trickling in, no valuables in the house. Just me and T-Rex here.' He pointed to the elderly Alsatian which slowly and briefly wagged its tail in recognition of its name and then settled back on to its blanket with a deep sigh.

'Can we see her room, please?'

'Certainly,' Beattie stood slowly and invited the officers to follow him. He led them along a long narrow corridor to a flight of wooden stairs. Both officers felt that the house could only be described as 'depressing'. It was dark, cold, and had decades-old wallpaper peeling from the walls. It seemed to the officers that the deeper Beattie led them into the house the more depressing it became.

'It's a matter of pride,' Beattie explained as, with evident difficulty, he climbed the stairs.

'What is, sir?'

'Not giving in to the cold. I just wear thermal underwear all the time, sometimes two layers. It does the job pleasingly well. Mrs Beattie felt the same. In the depths of winter we would put up camp beds in the kitchen, the old cast iron range we used for cooking retained its warmth well into the night, you see; warmer than being upstairs in the bedroom. Very efficient. I still use the same method to get through the cold days. Not cold any more ... winter has gone ... I sleep in my bedroom these nights.'

'You don't think this is cold, sir?' Yellich felt the chill within the house reach his bones.

'No ... nowhere near, the cut-off point is when your breath condenses in the house; we are a long way from that point. We just have to get through this late frost and then it will be spring.' He turned at the top of the staircase and led Yellich and Webster along a narrow corridor of creaking bare floorboards with a single window at the end of it; a naked light bulb hung forlornly from a black entwined electric cable just inside the window. 'That's the light I keep on to let the old boy who lives across the fields know that I am still alive. I'll switch it on when it gets dark.' He stopped by a door and opened it. 'This was her room.' He stepped aside.

Yellich and Webster entered the room and saw that it was spartan in the extreme. It contained a single metal framed bed with a hard looking mattress, a small wardrobe of perhaps the 1930s in terms of its age and a chest of drawers of what seemed to the officers to be of the same vintage. There was also a dressing table with a mirror attached to it and an upright chair in front of it. The floorboards, like the corridor outside the room, were without covering. The room was illuminated by a single light bulb which, similar to the light bulb in the corridor, was naked and hung from the ceiling at the end of a length of entwined electric cable of the type used in houses prior to the Second World War. There was no source of heating in the room. The window looked out across the fields at the front of the house to the road and to the hills beyond the road.

'Do you see what I mean?' Beattie said triumphantly. 'I mean about the French Foreign Legion Syndrome. Who would accept this accommodation unless they had to? She was on the run all right. It should have made both me and my son suspicious.'

'Seems so.' Yellich looked at the cell-like

room in the isolated prison-like house. He thought Beattie to be correct. Only a very frightened person would accept live-in accommodation of this low standard. There was not even a lock on the door. He asked if anyone visited her.

'No ... not a visitor, no one called on her ... but ... since you mention it...'

'But?' Yellich pressed.

'There was the large bearded man. I saw him a few times standing on the edge of the road, just looking at the house. I do not often look out of the house and so he was probably there more often than the three times I saw him.'

'That's interesting.' Yellich spoke softly, looking out of the window of the room. 'Was Edith ... or Julia ... in the house at the time, can you recall?'

'It was about the time she left, a few months ago, come to think of it. I well recall I mentioned it to her, that is to say that I had seen a man standing by the road looking at the house. She seemed worried by the information. Then she left. But she was planning to leave anyway. She had been emptying my bank account for weeks before I saw the man for the first time. Perhaps his arrival was just coincidence. Perhaps she thought she had taken me for all she could and was going to make tracks anyway ... but she did seem frightened when I described him to her.'

'Can you describe him for us now? Can you remember his appearance?'

'Well, the eyesight isn't what it used to be. He was a large man, bearded, like I said, solidly built. He wore a fur hat.'

'A fur hat?'

'Yes. A man's fur hat, like you see Russian soldiers wearing.'

'I know the type.'

'Light coloured. Not dark, so Arctic fox, not rabbit fur.'

'And not frightened of being seen?'

'No, he wasn't, now you mention it. He did not seem to care if he was seen. Red jacket ... tartan pattern.'

'Seems like someone we ought to talk to; he obviously had some interest in the house.' Yellich turned to Webster who nodded in agreement.

'You could try my neighbour,' Beattie suggested.

'Really?'

'Yes, he saw him once, driving past very slowly. He got a good look at him. He'll be able to give you more details than I can.' Beattie stepped into the room and opened a drawer in the dressing table. 'We kept all the stuff about her in here.' He took out the reference and read it. 'Look at what he said, that fox hunter type, "Industrious and utterly trustworthy". Tosh! But he got rid of her and here...' he took another piece of paper from the drawer, 'is the crime number I mentioned, given to me in respect of the theft of my money and valuables.' He handed it to Yellich.

'Malton Police.' Yellich read the slip of paper.

'Yes, that's the local bobby shop around here. Still a fair few miles away but it's the local cop shop.'

'You don't need it?'

'No, I can't claim for the lost money, I verified that with the insurance people, only for items, and she didn't steal much from the house because there was little to steal. She took some of Mrs Beattie's jewellery ... that I would like back but the value of the other stuff was minimal. Valuable only in terms of sentimental value … but I refer to them as the "valuables".'

'He's a tight-fisted old thing.' Ben Tinsley stood defensively in the doorway of his house. 'Dare say he has little good to say about me but do you know that in the wintertime he sleeps on a camp bed in his kitchen rather than have a heater in his bedroom, him and his wife also when she was with us? But we're both getting on and we are neighbours, and so I keep an eye on him and he keeps an eye on me.'

'Yes,' Yellich smiled, 'he told us the system you have of leaving a light burning to let each other know you are well. Also of moving his Land Rover about. A good idea.'

'Not uncommon in the country. But do please come in out of the cold, gentlemen.'

In contrast to Alexander Beattie's home, Yellich and Webster found Ben Tinsley's home was small, warm and dry. A settled coal fire burned gently in the grate.

'Not legal,' Tinsley pointed to the fire, and did so with clear embarrassment.

'I know.' Yellich read the room, photographs of family on the wall and mantelpiece, a compact television and a pile of magazines about walking in the country and coarse fishing. A physically fit widower, fond of his family, living within his means, enjoying solitary pursuits: nothing for the officers to be at all suspicious about. 'But we won't report you.'

'Thank you. This is the country, I am not polluting anyone else's breathing air and there is nothing like a coal fire. You just can't beat coal for a home fire. Take it from me, you just can't beat a coal fire. Do take a seat, please.'

The officers sat in deep comfortable armchairs covered with flower patterned material.

'So how can I help you?' Tinsley sat on a matching sofa. 'I saw you at Beattie's house, house ... mausoleum more like, if you ask me. I mean, what is he proving living in such cold conditions? He sees it as an achievement to get through the winter without heating, miserly old fool that he is. I tell you, he is the sort of man who would buy a poppy for one Remembrance Sunday, pay next to nothing for it and wear it for the next ten

Remembrance Sundays until it falls apart, then he buys another one for a penny or two and wears that for the first week in each November until that too falls apart, and so on and so forth. That's Beattie, claiming poverty but I bet he has a pile tucked away somewhere. Anyway I knew you were cops so I didn't interfere.'

'You knew?' Webster asked.

'Yes. You looked confident, were a pair and calling during the hours of daylight. Also you are both in good physical shape. But I took a few photographs of you anyway,' Tinsley smiled.

'You did?'

'Yes I did. Just in case. And I also made sure I got your car registration in one of the shots. I used a telephoto lens, you see, then I saw Beattie invite you into his house ... so I relaxed.'

'Good for you.'

'I'll send prints of them to you when I develop the film. Malton Police Station?'

'No. York. Micklegate Bar. But we'd still like to see them.'

'Really? York Police, I mean...'

'Yes, really.'

'All right. So, how can I help you?' Tinsley sat back on the sofa, 'I am intrigued.'

'Mr Beattie advised us that once a bearded man in a fur hat and tartan patterned jacket seemed to paying a lot of interest in his house. This was a couple of years ago, or so. He also said you may have got a look at him.'

'The Canadian? Yes ... but that's going back a good few months now, nearly two years, as you say ... time flies so.'

'Tell us about him, if you would,' Yellich asked. 'All you can remember.'

'What is there to say?' Tinsley sighed. 'Little to tell,' he paused as the clock in his hallway chimed the hour with the Westminster chimes. 'I used to see him in the village, that is Stillington, closest village to here, I really knew him from there. He used to enjoy a beer in The Hunter's Moon.'

'The Hunter's Moon in Stillington?' Webster wrote in his notebook.

'On the high street, you can't miss it. It was Terry the publican who told me he was a Canadian; they had a chat now and again, you see. Terry's good like that, he checks out strangers but does so in a friendly, chatty way. But yes, he was a Canadian. Tall, well built, beard, as you say, and yes, I saw him on the roadway just staring at Beattie's ruin and also I saw as he drove past in his car. He was clearly hanging around the area. The building had some fascination for him, it really did. That house, Beattie could have bought an easily run, warm, comfortable house but they bought that ... ruin ... no wonder his wife didn't last, but he seems to be sticking it out, stubborn old fool that he is. I tell you, if he were a plant he'd be moss which grows in the tundra, thriving in the cold. But the Canadian, he was a married man ... I can tell you that.'

'Married?'

'Yes. High quality clothes, had a car ... probably a hire car, it was the sort bought in large numbers by fleet operators. He hung around for a couple of weeks, so he must have stayed somewhere local and he didn't look like the youth hostel type. He wasn't frightened of being seen, that was something else about him, just standing there, as though he possibly even wanted to be seen.'

'Intimidating? Would you say it was an intimidating gesture on his part?'

Tinsley pursed his lips, 'Yes ... yes, I dare

say that you could say that. Intimidating.'

'But you never spoke to him?'

'No. Drove past him so got a closer look ... then later I saw him in the village once or twice ... heard about him from the boys in The Hunter's Moon. I'd try there if I was you.'

'I think we will. Thank you ... that's very helpful.'

'You might have to knock on the door.'

'At this hour!' Yellich grinned. 'He'll have been open since eleven a.m.'

'He would if he was in the centre of York, but these are getting to be hard times, pubs in the country can't pay if they open each day all day. Sometimes it's weekend trade only ... especially lately.'

'I see,' Yellich nodded his head slowly. 'Well, thanks anyway. Enjoy your fire.'

George Hennessey once again read the inscription beneath the names on the war memorial inside the doors of the central post office in York, 'Pass friend, all's well', as he exited the building, and was once again moved by it. He stepped out into a mist-laden street and strolled along Stonegate to

99

the Minster where he saw the tops of all three square towers were hidden from view, and the building itself seemed, in the diminishing light, to have taken on an eerie and foreboding presence. Foot traffic was light and seemed to Hennessey to be local people in the main, hurrying about their business, with just one or two very evident tourists staring in awe at the Minster, or in fascination at the Roman remains, or at the ancient buildings close by.

In the shadow of the Minster two women played musical instruments for passing change. The first woman was in her early twenties, tall, slender, wearing expensive looking footwear and equally expensive looking outer clothing. She played a violin and to Hennessey's ear did so impressively well. She had, Hennessey observed, been blessed with classical good looks and her blonde hair draped over her shoulders which moved slightly from side to side as her slender and nimble fingers danced along the neck of the violin and her other hand gently held the bow which she moved lightly, but at speed, across the strings. She was, by her countenance, utterly focused. The black bowler hat at her feet was, Hennessey noted, understandably full of coins and even one or two five pound notes. The second woman sat a few feet behind the violinist, in the doorway of a temporarily vacant shop unit. She huddled in a blanket and picked out 'Edelweiss' from *The Sound of Music* on a cheap tin whistle. The plastic cup in front of her contained few, very few, low denomination coins. Her demeanour was, assessed Hennessey, one of detachment. She played mechanically, he thought, but her mind was elsewhere. His urge was to place an appreciative coin or two in the bowler hat but he paused as he pondered the clear privilege of birth of the violinist. She seemed to him to be the product of an expensive education and certainly was busking to ease the financial burden of her university course, and York University, at that; one of England's finest. Her clothing, her violin, the music stand, even the bowler hat on the paving stones at her feet all spoke of wealth. Hennessey found himself becoming intrigued by the drawn and haggard-faced tin whistle player and so he walked towards her and dropped a pound coin in her plastic cup. The woman's eyes widened at his generosity and she looked up at him as if to say 'Thank you', to which Hennessey said, 'Let me buy you a coffee.'

The woman stopped playing. 'A coffee?'

'I could run to a late lunch. When did you last eat?'

'Two days ago ... and not much then ... a cup of soup and some bread.'

'Let's get some hot food inside you. I think we'd better.'

'Would you?' she gasped her reply.

'Yes, I would. You can leave your blanket here. If you fold it neatly no one will take it away.'

The woman, who seemed to Hennessey to be in her mid to late thirties, struggled awkwardly to her feet, out of the blanket. She was dressed in damp looking denim with a red corduroy shirt and inexpensive looking and well worn running shoes.

Hennessey took her to a nearby cafe and they sat at the window seat. The woman received a hostile look from the middle-aged waitress, which Hennessey noticed, and he replied to it with an angry glare which forced the waitress into a hasty retreat. She sent another waitress to take Hennessey's order. 'So,' Hennessey said, 'tell me about yourself.'

'Where do I begin?'

'Your name might be a good place.'

'You sound like a cop.'

'That's probably because I am a cop.'

'I thought you were.'

'It's written on my forehead, I know.'

The woman smiled softly. 'I have nothing to hide.'

'I didn't think you had.'

'So why the meal?'

'You are helping yourself. I am impressed. I respect that.'

'Thanks, but I am not very good. I needed to play "three identifiable tunes", that's the rule ... in order to get my street entertainer's licence. I found the whistle in a charity shop for a few pence and learned to play 'Edelweiss', 'Bobby Shaftoe' and 'Three Blind Mice'...we had lessons on a recorder when I was at secondary school. It was good enough, just good enough to get my licence ... so I play the three tunes over and over again and bank on the assumption that no one will walk past me twice so no one will hear the same tune from me twice.'

'But good for you...'

The conversation paused as the waitress brought two platefuls of shepherd's pie and chips with a pot of tea for two.

'Well, I tried to sell the flesh but I wasn't very good at it ... couldn't go through with it.'

'Good,' Hennessey smiled, 'I'm pleased you avoided that ... never leads a girl anywhere but trouble.'

'Hardly a girl, I was thirty-six when I tried it.'

'Even so ... anyway, you still haven't told me your name.'

'Tilly Pakenham.'

'Tilly?'

'Short for Matilda. Sounds posh but it's not, not like the violinist, she's posh. My dad is a bus driver ... we lived in a council house.'

'You could have fooled me. You have a pleasant speaking voice.'

'It's true ... the speaking voice was acquired by listening to Radio Four, the old self-improvement number ... went well until I fell from grace.'

'What happened?' Hennessey glanced

round the cafe. He had not been in it before, it was of new design and did not try to evoke 'the old'. It had a large window fronting on to the street, metal tables with metal chairs, it was light, airy, spacious, the food was of a reasonable quality, he thought, and the portions were generous. The disapproving reaction of the first waitress to Matilda Pakenham's presence had been, thus far, the only unpleasant aspect.

'What do you think? Why do so many women fall from grace?' She imitated shooting herself in the head. 'Bad choice of husband, that is the sort of mistake that can carry a long way in any woman's life. Are you married?'

'Long time widower.'

'I'm sorry.'

'Well, as I said, a long time widower. All adjustments have been made. So, carry on...'

'He was just a no-good, my parents said so the instant they saw him. "Dangerous and no good" was my mother's reaction ... and women's intuition being what it is ... and boy was she right or was she right...? He was a charming man but also a violent control freak.'

Hennessey nodded as he stirred his tea. 'I know the type; the jails are full of them.'

'I was his possession, not his wife. He's a salesman ... film star looks ... the patter ... the eye contact, the charm ... he can make it work and he's good at his job ... he makes sales ... but once I was present when he got sour with a customer who then said, "Well, you've changed your tune", to which he replied, "I'm only nice if you buy something from me".'

'Blimey,' Hennessey gasped.

'Yes, that's him; his surname is even Smiley ... how appropriate. Anyway things just happened once too often and so I walked out.'

'Good for you.'

'Went back to using my maiden name but I am too proud to return home.'

'Which is where?'

'Northampton ... sunny Northampton. It's just one of those towns you pass through on your way to somewhere interesting but it's where my roots are. It's home and the one place I cannot go.'

'You could visit. It's not too far away ... ease yourself back in...'

'I could, it's near enough and far enough,

which is how I like it, but he's looking for me. He didn't like losing his possession like that, took it as a personal insult.'

'He is?'

'Yes.' Matilda Pakenham sipped her tea. 'Oh ... that's nice,' she sighed. 'The English and their tea ... but it does have medicinal qualities, it does have more ... more ... uplift than coffee, I find anyway.'

'Yes...'

'I went to Cambridge when I first left, because of the year-round tourist trade, and that's where I found my tin whistle in a charity shop. Then he found me, slapped me around a bit and pushed me into his car and took me home to where we lived in Grantham and slapped me around a bit more and I escaped again and came to York with a blanket and me old tin whistle.'

'More year-round tourists?'

'That was the idea but he's here looking for me.'

'How does he know that you are here?'

'He'll work it out, he knows about me sitting in doorways playing on the tin tube ... knows I don't like going too far from Northampton ... he'll work it out. You know I really believe that I can feel his presence; I can feel him in the air. A few days ago I was walking home from my pitch and I stopped in my tracks and said, "He's here".'

'Interesting. Do you have any children?'

'No, thank heavens. I'd like a couple, what woman doesn't? But not by him. So I dare say I am lucky in that respect ... just me and him ... things could be an awful lot more complicated.'

'Well,' Hennessey took a business card from his wallet and handed it to Matilda Pakenham, 'we can't do anything unless you press charges.'

'I know, but he's careful not to slap me in front of witnesses and keeps me locked up until all the bruises have faded.'

'Yes, I know the score ... but we can offer protection.'

'OK,' she slipped the card into her shirt pocket. 'Thank you, Mr Hennessey.'

'George,' Hennessey smiled. 'Call me George.'

'It's the economic depression, you see.' The man, Roger Blackwood by the nameplate on his desk and by his warm introduction, was a slightly built man, smartly, very smartly dressed and with, Thomson Ventnor found, a very serious attitude. So serious that he guessed it would take much to make the man smile. 'Those units have been empty for about eighteen months. We haven't recovered our money. We built them and let them out. All of them. Then the economy took a downturn and the tenants' businesses folded and they vacated the premises as a consequence of that and we have not been able to re-let them. We will just have to wait for the upswing. Someone forced entry, you say?'

'It appears so, to Unit Five.'

'Business is bad. I don't think the boss will pay for that to be repaired, not in a hurry anyway, but they are so out of the way that that might not be a problem and there is nothing to steal anyway ... nothing to burn and nothing to vandalize. I think the company will live with the damage until the upswing comes.'

'I see, but we are more interested in the location than the damage.'

'Why?' Blackwood inclined his head. 'What's afoot?'

'Because of the remoteness.'

'Nothing special about that. The cheap land is reflected in the low rents.'

'I can understand that.'

'Unpopular place to work though, very unpopular. One firm had to bus its employees in; no facilities for the workforce during the day, nowhere to spend their lunch breaks ... especially in the winter. All the workforce could do was shelter and eat their packed lunches. Then the businesses all went bust anyway.'

'Yes, but the remoteness suggests local knowledge.'

'You think so?'

'We believe it might ... it's a distinct possibility.'

'Frankly, I think the remoteness doesn't imply local knowledge. It doesn't imply anything at all.'

Thomson Ventnor groaned as he sensed a promising lead evaporate.

'A bit of research, I would have thought, a bit of exploration, a glance at a map ... just driving about looking for an out-of-the-way place,' Blackwood explained, 'or anyone could just have stumbled upon the site.'

It was, conceded Ventnor, a fair and reasonable argument. Local knowledge could not be safely implied. He glanced round Blackwood's office within the offices of The Ouse, Derwent and Trent Property Company. He saw it to be small, cramped even, but made more bearable by what he thought was intelligent use of available space. He looked out of the window at Stonebow. All concrete and glass. A modern part of the ancient city and not at all to his liking. Parts of ancient York could only be in York but Stonebow was, he often argued, any town in Western Europe.

'I would think the location would have to be researched. What's the word? Some reconnaissance would have had to be done, but that's your business, I do not want to intrude, not really my place to do so. Would need strength though.'

'Strength?'

'Yes, I would have thought so. The units were left well secured despite the remoteness of the location ... heavy duty chain and very large padlocks. It would need a bolt cutter and some muscle to get through them.'

'Good point, I'll pass that up,' Ventnor smiled. 'Has anyone expressed an interest in renting one of the units? Wanting to view them ... very recently?'

'No and I would have known, any such request would have landed here.' Roger Blackwood patted the top of his desk. 'Those units are in my portfolio which is why you are talking to me, not another under manager. So, no, no recent interest.'

'Thank you anyway,' Ventnor stood, 'just covering all our bases.'

'Of course ... you'll be paying for the damage of course ... where do we send the invoice?'

'What damage?'

'Well, following your phone call I took a quick trip out there to see what was going on.'

'Yes...?'

'And all the units had been forced open. Now new chains and locks will be needed ... so where do we send the invoice?'

'Well, one person was held in one of the units against her will, we had to check them all ... no time to get warrants or find the key holder ... life might have been at risk. So, no, we won't be paying for any damage. Good day.'

* * *

Hennessey drove sedately home. It was a little early for him to leave Micklegate Bar Police Station but an officer of his rank was permitted a little fluidity in timekeeping in recognition of the extra hours he often, very often, worked. With Yellich and Webster still out visiting there was, he reasoned, little else he could do that day and so he enjoyed an early finish. Upon entering Easingwold and finding the town quiet, he stopped his car on Long Street where the houses and shops were joined, each with the other, to form a continuous roofline along the length of the road. He walked with a heavy heart to where she had fallen, all those years ago, a young woman in the very prime of her life, just three months after the birth of her first child, the first of a planned three for her and her husband George. She had collapsed. Suddenly. People rushed to her aid assuming she had fainted but no pulse could be found. She was declared dead on arrival at the hospital, or Condition Purple, in ambulance speak. Her post-mortem findings led the coroner to rule that she had died of Sudden Death Syndrome, which, Hennessey had

113

come to learn, attacks young people in their twenties and who are in excellent health, causing the life within them to leave as if a light had been switched off and switched at random, and for no clear purpose. Hennessey, holding his three-month-old son in one arm, had used the other to scatter Jennifer's ashes on the rear lawn of their home in Easingwold, and had then set about rebuilding the garden according to the design she had carefully drawn whilst heavily pregnant with Charles. George Hennessey never thought his wife was here, in Long Street, but felt her presence to be in the garden at the rear of their house. Even as a widower of a cruelly short marriage he always thought that he lived in 'their' house and, at the end of each day's work, no matter what the weather, he would stand on the rear patio and tell Jennifer about his day. During the previous summer he had also told her of a new relationship in his life, whilst assuring her that his love for her was not and never would be diminished, and then he had felt a warmth surround him which could not be explained as coming from the sun alone. It was something deeper, something much,

much richer and something very specific to him and him alone.

Carmen Pharoah got out of her car as she saw Stanley Hemmings amble in a lost, dream-like state towards his house. He cut, she thought, a helpless and a hapless figure – small with a battered look about him. He forced a smile when she showed him her ID.

'Didn't expect you, Miss, sorry. I just went out for a walk; don't know what to do now our Edith is no more. Now she's gone before. Just feel too alone in the house so I go out and walk round, can't seem to stay settled. I'll go back to work soon, that'll keep my mind occupied.'

'No matter, I thought I'd wait to see if you returned.'

'Do come in, please.' He walked up the drive of his house, past a small red van from which 'EIIR' had been removed from the sides but a trace of the lettering remained. Ex-Post Office van, deduced Pharoah, most likely bought at an auction. 'One day I'll go and see where she was held ... when you tell me where that is.'

'Keeping it to ourselves for the time being,

sir. Don't want to contaminate the crime scene any.'

'Oh, yes, like on television ... I watch those television programmes.'

'Yes.'

'I laid a bunch of flowers on the canal bank, though, assumed that was all right.'

'Yes,' Carmen Pharoah smiled, 'no harm done there. The principal crime scene is where Mrs Hemmings was held captive.'

Hemmings put his hand inside his jacket pocket and took out a house key. 'Do come in, Miss,' he repeated as he unlocked and opened the door. Pharoah noticed how the key turned smoothly in a well lubricated lock. 'Sorry about the mess, I haven't tidied up for a bit, didn't realize how much my wife did until I had to do it all myself.'

'No matter.' Carmen Pharoah stepped up the step and over the threshold and into the small kitchen. 'You should see the houses we have to visit from time to time.'

'I can imagine.'

'The reason I have been asked to call is that I wonder if it's possible for us, the police, to look at Mrs Hemmings's personal possessions?'

'Yes, of course … by all means.' Hemmings peeled off his jacket, reached for the kettle and filled it with water from the tap, and did so as if on autopilot, Carmen Pharoah observed, as if in a state of shock or as if a lifetime's habit was to boil a kettle of water immediately upon returning home. 'Her room is the back bedroom. Please...' he indicated the hallway which led to the stairs.

'Her room? You don't … you didn't...?'

'No,' he turned to her with an icy expression, 'we didn't share a marital bed. Not lately anyway. We had an understanding, you see. It suited us both.'

'I see. Can I go up?'

'Yes,' Hemmings lit the gas ring and placed the kettle upon it, 'the back bedroom … that is … that was Edith's room.'

Carmen Pharoah climbed the narrow stairway of the house and entered the rear bedroom. She encountered a musty smell within the room which had only a single unmade bed, a wardrobe and a dressing table. Carmen Pharoah pondered the unmade bed. Had Mrs Hemmings departed with some urgency? Did her husband care so little for her, despite his apparent grief, that he did not go into her room at all? When she was a missing person, making up her bed in anticipation of her return would have been the act of a worried and caring husband, or so Carmen Pharoah would have thought, but was it in fact the case that the quality of their marriage had deteriorated to the point that they were banned from each other's room? Perhaps ... perhaps ... perhaps. Carmen Pharoah walked across the threadbare carpet to the dressing table. It seemed to her to be a sensible place to start looking, though she did not know what exactly she was searching for. Upon the table, in front of the mirror, was an array of cosmetics and a few items of jewellery, all of which she classed as 'mid range'. Nothing there indicated wealth, nor equally of her struggling finances. It was, it seemed, fully in keeping with the house, a modest, three bedroom semi owned by a supervisor in the biscuit factory. Just Dringhouses, York. Comfortable. And mid range items within.

In the drawer of the dressing table she found Edith Hemmings's birth certificate which put her age at forty-seven years, her birthplace as Ottawa, Canada and her maiden name as Aurillé. Also in the drawer she found a Canadian passport in the name of Edith Avrillé. The passport was still valid. Mr Hemmings had probably been her first husband although Carmen Pharoah knew that obtaining a passport in one's maiden name, or renewing a passport in a woman's maiden name, was not an uncommon practice, nor was it particularly difficult. She replaced the passport and took hold of a hardback notebook within which were written musings and overused sayings, 'Don't light a fire you can't put out' and 'Pain is temporary but failure lasts a lifetime' being but two. Also in the book were a number of addresses: St Joseph's, Riddeau Terrace, Ottawa; Liff and Company, Barrie, Ontario; forty-three Allison Heights, Barrie; nineteen Wilbury Street, Barrie, Ontario. Carmen Pharoah felt it safe to disregard the single line entreaties to Edith Hemmings striving for common sense and proceeded to copy down all the addresses in the notebook. She then opened the wardrobe, rummaged through the clothing, felt her way across the top of the shelf in the wardrobe and, finding nothing else of promising significance, returned downstairs. She found Stanley Hemmings still in the kitchen, sipping a cup of tea. 'I have all I need,' she told him, calmly.

'Oh. What are you taking?' Hemmings sounded alarmed.

'Nothing. I am leaving everything where I found it. I have seen the birth certificate and passport and found her notebook; I have made a few notes but left everything in its proper place. We would ask you to do the same. Please do not clear the room, not just yet.'

'Yes, understood. I won't. I'll be cremating her, by the way.'

'Sorry?'

'I'll be cremating her. Just thought you might be interested or would want to know. They have released the body.'

'I see ... yes, the post-mortem was conclusive.'

'Yes ... so they cut her up so much it just seems the right thing to do is to cremate her. She won't rest at peace with her insides cut open. She was neat like that. Liked things just so, did our Edith.'

'Have you anybody to keep an eye on you,

Mr Hemmings, to look in on you at a time like this?'

'At a time like this I am best on my own, but thank you very much for your concern. Best back to work in my brown smock ... but again, thank you for your concern, Miss. I appreciate it,' he added with a weak smile.

Carmen Pharoah let herself out of the house and walked slowly back to where she had parked her car, feeling a strange sense that she had visited emptiness.

'He's right.' Terry Selsey, proprietor of The Hunter's Moon, leaned on the highly polished bar of the pub, having handed a coffee each to Yellich and Webster. 'It's the recession, you see. This is a struggling pub at the best of times. It struggled when I opened for seven days a week, when folk had money to spend, and I just kept my head above water, but only just. Then customers stopped coming in and the hard times began. I had to let staff go, one by one, and now me and the wife run it between us. Just the two of us. We tried everything to lure the punters in, put on food but nobody had the money to eat out. Lowered the price of the beer until we were virtually selling it at cost but still nobody came in. So now we don't open until eight p.m. Friday, Saturday and Sunday and even then it's like this most of the time.' He nodded to the empty chairs and to the silence. 'I'd even welcome a fight to break up because that would mean there were customers in the place ... that it should come to thinking like that.'

'I know what you mean.' Yellich stirred his coffee.

'Do you?' Selsey snarled. 'You with your security of employment, early retirement at fifty-five years, inflation-proof pension ... do you know what I mean?' Selsey's eyebrows knitted. He was clearly, thought Yellich, a man with a short fuse.

'I meant,' Yellich replied calmly, 'I knew what you meant about wanting a fight to break up because that meant you had customers in the pub.' He thought Selsey to be like many publicans he had met. He was a man with a ready smile, superficial joviality, but with the ability to turn and growl at the slightest provocation. It occurred to Yellich that a change in attitude on Selsey's part might generate a little more business for The

Hunter's Moon. 'So, the Canadian?' Yellich asked.

'Yes,' Selsey glanced to one side. 'He came in a few times, when we were busier; this is going back a couple of years mind. He went into the Black Bull further up the street as well but in the end he seemed to prefer this pub. The Bull is also a weekend-only shop now. Never caught his name but he seemed a likeable bloke, friendly when you talked to him, wore a wedding ring, but he definitely had an agenda.'

'An agenda?'

'Yes, by that I mean he wasn't on holiday or on vacation as he might have said. The Canadian, he was a man with a mission. He liked his English beer, though, drove away well over the legal limit but he could handle it. He had to go back to Malton.'

'Malton?'

'Yes, he said that once at about nine thirty one evening and he sank his pint in a hurry, as though he was under time pressure. I thought then that it was a good thirty minutes drive ... so he had to be home by ten, wherever "home" was, as though he was staying at a guest house which locked the doors at ten p.m. sharp.'

'All right. That's interesting. Did he ever indicate to you or anyone that you know of, did he ever hint at his purpose? I mean did he indicate the nature of the agenda you mention?'

'No ... not to me though he was apparently interested in the old house out of the village, the crumbling mess occupied by an old boy called Beattie. You can't miss it.'

'Yes, we have visited Mr Beattie. He also mentioned the large, well built man looking at his house but he thought that the Canadian, being the man in question, was more interested in the occupants than he was interested in the house itself.'

'Occupants? Since his wife died the old boy is the sole occupant, the old boy who is rumoured not to feel the cold ... they say he sleeps in his kitchen.'

'Oh, he feels it all right,' Yellich replied, 'he feels it, he just has a different attitude towards it than do the rest of us. We believe that when the Canadian was in the vicinity he, that is Mr Beattie, had a live-in help ... a lady ... as a domestic assistant. We believe that she was the object of the Canadian gentleman's interest.'

'Ah ... of that I know nothing. He said nothing about that when he was drinking his beer.'

'I see. Did he talk to any other customers in the pub?'

'Anybody who talked to him but he preferred his own company. He came in for a few beers, not idle chat. He was that sort of man.'

'Did you find out anything about him, anything at all?'

'Came from Barrie, he said. He did tell me that.'

'Barrie?'

'Confess I had never heard of the place, but it's north of Toronto. I could name Ottawa, Toronto, Montreal and Vancouver as Canadian cities but never heard of Barrie ... spelled with an "ie" at the end, not a "y".'

'Well, you got closer than anyone, physically closer, that is to say, and so we'd like you to help us construct a photofit of the man, or rather a computer generated image. What time would suit you?'

Selsey gave Yellich a sour look, 'If you could manage to avoid weekend evenings I'd appreciate it.'

'Later today perhaps?' Yellich suggested.
'Would that be convenient?'

Carmen Pharoah drove away from Stanley
Hemmings's house and then parked her car
and walked back the 200 yards and knocked
on his neighbour's door. Her knock sounded
loudly and hollowly within the house. As she
waited for the knock to be answered she
glanced at Hemmings's house. She did not
see him and thus was relieved that he clearly
had not seen her. If he had noticed her it
would not have mattered, but on balance,
she preferred him not to have seen her. It
made things easier somehow. The door was
eventually opened by a late middle-aged
woman, short, with a pinched face, who met
Carmen Pharoah with a cold stare and clear
dislike of Afro-Caribbeans.

'What?' She demanded. 'What is it? What
do you want? Who are you?'

'Police.' Carmen Pharoah showed the
woman her ID.

'Oh?' The woman seemed to relax her
attitude a little, though she still demanded
'What?' for a fourth time.

'May I come inside? I'd like to ask you some questions.' Carmen Pharoah asked calmly.

'About what?'

'Your neighbour.'

'Which neighbour?'

'Mr Hemmings.'

'Oh ... those two?' The woman sniffed disapprovingly.

'Yes, those two.'

The woman stepped nimbly to one side and allowed Carmen Pharoah to enter her house. Carmen Pharoah read a neat, well kept, clean but spartan home; hence, she realized, the echoing quality to her knock, there being little to soften the sound. 'Second on the left,' the woman said, closing the front door behind her.

Carmen Pharoah entered the living room which had upholstered furniture and a table covered in a brown cloth. Of daffodils in vases and a small television set in the corner of the room on a small table. A modest coke fire glowed dimly in the hearth. The window of the room looked out over a small but well tended rear garden and the wooden fence which divided her property from Stanley

Hemmings's property.

'Well, sit down,' the woman spoke snappily, 'the chairs don't bite.'

'Thank you.' Carmen Pharoah settled on the settee and opened her notepad. 'Can I ask your name, please?'

'Winterton. Amelia. Miss.'

'Occupation, please.'

'Schoolteacher, retired recently, a few months ago. Still don't know what to do with all my free time.'

Carmen Pharoah shuddered internally. She felt she knew the type of schoolteacher Winterton, Amelia, Miss, had been, acid-tongued, short-tempered. She had survived just one such teacher in her primary school on St Kitts.

'So, you are enquiring about the couple next door?'

'Yes ... yes, we are.'

'She disappeared I heard ... it's the talk of the street.'

'So we believe.'

'Oh, well, don't know what I can tell you ... probably not much at all. He was a long time bachelor and then he takes her for his wife. I don't think she was a happy woman.'

'Why do you say that? Did they argue?'

'No, I never heard any arguments or rows, nothing like that, not ever. She just didn't seem right for him. If you ask me they made an odd couple. You know Stanley, he works in the biscuit factory, harmless, kind old man, sort of character that you find in children's books, like the toymaker, and she ... sort of brash and materialistic. I just never saw her looking happy, if you see what I mean, and often going out alone ... separate ... by herself. But when we talked, over the back fence sort of chats, that is Stanley and I, I never talked to her, he just sang her praises all the time. Edith did this and Edith does that. He seemed so proud of her, but frankly I never saw her do anything ... good or bad. You know once I called round one Sunday morning because the brain-dead paperboy had delivered their newspapers to my address by mistake and he was in the kitchen in a pinafore very contentedly preparing Sunday lunch and I called again the same day and he was back in the pinafore equally contentedly doing the washing-up, and madam was just nowhere to be seen. He seemed to worship her and do everything in the house. She just scowled all the time.'

'I see.'

'Mind you, that Sunday I mention, in fairness that was just one day and so it might have been atypical. But I never saw her do any work. Never saw her weed the garden, put out the laundry on the line. She never brought shopping home, only him, only ever him in the garden, only ever him bringing the shopping home. She seemed to be content to stay in the house. They went out together occasionally in their little ex-post office van. She also wore a wig, she seemed to fancy being a blonde from time to time.'

'Yes ... the wig.'

'She would go out alone in the evening. That's something she did do, go out by herself. I heard her heels click, click, click away into the night and she'd return late at night. It was a strange union, ill-matched. I could never see what they saw in each other. He seems lost now though. You know I went round yesterday to see if he needed any help at this difficult time ... found him sobbing his eyes out ... poor man ... he must have loved her very much.'

★ ★ ★

Yellich and Webster returned to Micklegate Bar Police Station. Upon arrival they shared the recording to be added to the file of the murder of Edith Hemmings. Yellich recorded the longer interview with Alexander Beattie and Webster the two shorter interviews with Ben Tinsley and Terry Selsey.

Yellich then drove thankfully home to his new build house in Huntingdon to the north of York. He halted the car by the side of the road as Jeremy ran out of the house to greet him and Yellich braced himself for the impact of the heavy, and large for his age, twelve-year-old. Father and son walked hand in hand back to the house where Sara Yellich welcomed her husband with a warm smile and told him that Jeremy had been a very good boy since he returned home from school that afternoon. Later, when he had changed into more casual clothes, Somerled Yellich took Jeremy for a walk in the fields close to their home as a reward for being a good boy and they observed the beginning of spring, the snowdrops and crocuses, the first leaves on some species of tree ... and geese ... a skein of geese flying northwards against the grey sky.

Somerled and Sara Yellich had, like all couples in such circumstances, experienced feelings of disappointment when told that their son would not be of normal intelligence but would be deemed 'special needs'. In Jeremy Yellich's case the diagnosis being Down's Syndrome. But as Jeremy grew a new world opened up to them as they met other parents of similar children and formed real and lasting friendships with them. Jeremy too had given so much, developing as he had into a loving and trusting individual and one who would never be a source of angst to his parents as he grew into a teenager. For Jeremy Yellich the future would be of semi-independent living in a supervised hostel as he entered what might, sadly, be a short adult life with him achieving a mental age of approximately twelve years.

Later that evening Somerled and Sara Yellich sat with each other, resting against each other sipping wine and listening to Beethoven's 'Emperor' Concerto. There was just nothing they needed or had to say to each other.

THREE

Thursday, March twenty-sixth,
09.10 hours – Friday 02.00 hours
*in which a trail is followed, a revelation made,
and Reginald Webster and Thomson Ventnor are
separately at home to the kind reader.*

The drizzle turned slowly to snow as George Hennessey looked casually out of his office window and across the road to Micklegate Bar. He thought how it was that the weather made the walls of the ancient city look exceptionally cold and forbidding. He then turned to face the team assembled side by side in chairs in front of his desk forming a tight semicircle: Yellich, Webster, Ventnor and Pharoah. 'So,' he said as he relaxed in his chair, 'it appears that we need to trace the mysterious Canadian gentleman. He

133

seems to have some explaining to do.'

'Seems so, Skipper,' Yellich replied and then delicately sipped tea from the mug he was holding.

'So what do we think about Mr Stanley Hemmings? Is he in the frame?'

'He seems genuinely grief-stricken, sir.' Carmen Pharoah sat forward cradling her mug of tea in both hands. 'It did not sound like a blissfully happy union. He seems to have been besotted by her but ... it wasn't ... what's the word?' She appealed to her colleagues.

'Reciprocated?' Webster suggested. 'Is that the word you're looking for?'

'Yes, that's the very word. The passion seemed very one-sided, even allowing for their neighbour embellishing her own cynical view of things; Edith Hemmings did seem to be a bit of a handful of a woman. I did take her passport details so I can contact the Canadian authorities, although Mr Hemmings didn't indicate she had any relatives.'

'Yes, we must find out who she is ... was ... and determine her name; was she "Julia" or "Edith" and why did she seem so frightened of the Canadian gentleman who was looking for her? Something happened in Canada. Something very serious.'

'She was an orphan,' Yellich said, 'so we understand, at least according to Mr Beattie, though some relatives may exist, some extended family.'

'Yes, we have to involve the Canadians. That's one for you, DC Pharoah...'

'Yes, sir.'

'There is nothing to report in respect of the industrial units,' Ventnor reported. 'I visited them yesterday, a struggling property company. The units have been empty for some time, quite isolated but also easily stumbled across. How he found them is a question we'll likely put to the Canadian when we catch up with him. Seems he is our man, stalking Mrs Hemmings like he did, over a number of years. We really need to find him.'

Hennessey paused. 'So, time for action. DC Pharoah, contact the Canadian Embassy as you suggested. What else have you got on?'

'Two serious assaults, sir, both domestic, and I am helping the CPS to frame charges against a serial shoplifter, "Liz the lifter" as she is known, and prolific isn't the word and that's just going on what we know. What we don't know about would probably fill Marks and Spencer's twice over ... and she's still only seventeen.'

'We'll be getting to know her very well,' Hennessey smiled.

'Indeed, sir ... very well indeed.'

'Sergeant?'

'Fatal stabbing in the city centre, sir, not far from here ... by the cholera burial pits. The felon is in custody and will be pleading guilty. His brief is trying to negotiate a reduced charge but we'll get a result one way or the other. Other than that I have much paperwork to do.'

'OK. Ventnor?'

'Car thefts in the main, sir. Seems like an organized gang is behind them, they are targeting high value prestige motors, but there has been nothing for six weeks now, unless they have moved on to another city. So it's become a waiting game.'

'Very well. Webster?'

'Burglaries in the main, sir, and also possibly one very well organized gang ... and again, it's also a waiting game. They'll slip up one day but these fellas are very clever, very thorough. They seem to be well aware that every contact leaves a trace ... so very careful ... most carefully not wanting to cut themselves it seems, so as not to leave DNA behind ... clean breaking of panes of glass has become their hallmark.'

'Right,' Hennessey sat forward, 'so Webster and Yellich, I want you two to team up. Find this damned Canadian and find out more about the victim. She came from somewhere and he has gone somewhere. Pursue both lines of enquiry. At some point they will converge.'

'Yes, sir,' Yellich replied promptly.

'For myself, I intend to visit a gentleman who has been helpful before. I doubt he will know the Canadian man but he might know Mrs Hemmings. If she has been stealing from her employers in the Vale for a number of years then my man will probably know her. Was the date of entry stamped on her passport?'

'No, sir.'

'No matter. So the other place of employment she had before she worked for Beattie ... that will have to be visited, and we also need to find the guest house he used when he was in the area.'

'Yes, sir.'

'Well, leave it to you two gentlemen to see what you see and to find what you find.'

'It's been over two years now, confess it seems like it was yesterday. Damned woman ... I feel that this house was contaminated by her.'

The address of the man who had employed Edith Hemmings née Avrillé and whose character reference Alexander Beattie described as a 'work of convincing fiction' revealed itself to be a large and a lovingly tended property set in its own grounds with stables adjoining the main building. Other outbuildings were visible, including a large greenhouse development. Upon halting the car on the gravel in front of the house and drawing back the metal ring pull by the front door, Yellich and Webster were greeted leisurely by an elderly butler. The man wore a dark jacket with grey pinstriped trousers and highly polished shoes. He was clearly a man with a serious attitude to his position and closely examined the IDs of both offi-

.cers. He then invited Yellich and Webster into the house, showing them into a large wood panelled foyer in which a log fire crackled and burned welcomingly in a cast iron grate within a stone built fireplace. He then asked the officers to wait and excused himself. The fire seemed to speak to the officers of emotional warmth as well as of a very welcome heat. The foyer was further softened by two large, highly polished brass pots which stood either side of the door and within each of which a thriving yucca plant was established. The foyer smelled of wood smoke mingling with furniture polish.

The butler returned after an absence of about five minutes, Webster guessed, and he warmly and politely invited the officers into an anteroom softly but tastefully furnished with armchairs and a table surrounded by upright chairs. The room, Yellich and Webster noted, was smaller than the foyer but was similarly appointed with wood panelling and had an equally welcoming log fire burning in a cast iron grate. Oil paintings of rural scenes hung on the wall. The butler invited the officers to sit, saying, 'Mr Rigall will be with you shortly.'

'Shortly' transpired to be very short. In fact no more than sixty seconds after Yellich and Webster were left in the room to await Mr Rigall, the man entered. He was tall, powerfully built, dressed in faded denim jeans and a blue shirt over which he wore a large, sloppy woollen cardigan. He was clean shaven, short-haired and he smelled of aftershave. Webster and Yellich stood as he entered the room and he waved them to resume their seats. Rigall apologized for keeping them waiting, explaining in a soft voice that he had been under the shower when they called. 'I am a bit of a late riser,' he added by means of explanation. 'How can I help you?'

Webster explained the reason for their visit.

Rigall groaned and sank into a leather clad armchair. He then said, 'It's been two years now ... confess it seems like it was yesterday. Damn woman.'

'Tell us about her ... please,' Yellich asked, as Webster took his notebook from his jacket.

'Where to start?' He twisted his body and took a packet of cigarettes from his jeans

140

pocket. 'Sorry ... do you mind?'

'Not at all, sir.'

'Would either of you gentlemen like a cigarette?'

'No, thank you, sir,' Webster said as Yellich gave his head a brief shake, and added. 'Thank you anyway, sir.'

'Sensible. Wish I didn't but with my wife no longer here to tell me off I have picked up quite a few bad habits, this being one such. I manage the estate and have some business interests but you know, I confess I quite enjoyed surrendering my everyday life to my wife's control, it seemed to take the pressure off me when I came home ... and she had a strict "no smoking" rule so I observed it. It was her house and she was the boss. It would not suit all men but it suited me.' He lit the cigarette with an inexpensive blue coloured disposable lighter. 'We were an odd couple in many regards. She was a small, quick woman who could be sharp-tongued and very quick-tempered when it suited her. I do not apologize for it, I am well built and much slower moving than she was, much calmer in my attitude. We were yang and yin. We were just like a hand and a glove.' He drew deeply on the cigarette. 'She died suddenly in a riding accident ... sorry to ramble but I promise that it all builds up to explaining how the Canadian creature came to live here. It is the background.'

'Yes, sir,' Webster replied, gently sensing that Tony Rigall also needed to tell them the story for his own highly personal reasons.

'No one saw the accident. Her horse found its way back to the stables whinnying in distress ... snorting and neighing ... heavens, the damn thing actually raised the alarm. She and her horse loved each other; there was a real bond there, a real relationship. Any other beast would have just stood there chewing the grass waiting for someone to lead it home, but "Scarlet" – her horse, she had a distinct reddish tinge on her flank, hence her name – Scarlet galloped home, back to the stables, and raised the alarm. Two of the estate workers followed her back to where my wife was lying motionless on the ground.' He paused. 'Anyway, she was DOA at the hospital. It was a blessing. There is such a thing as a "quality of life". She was thirty-five, still a young woman. The fracture was high up on the spine near the base of the neck. One vertebra lower and she would have been a tetraplegic, paralysed from the neck down and with another forty plus years of life left to live. Trapped on a lifeless body, her head would have been perched on the top of a vegetable. She was very physical, horse riding, swimming, cross-country running, hill walking, you name it ... all on top of managing the house. She had a way with the staff; she could inspire them to want to work for her, she was a natural leader. She ran a very peaceful and efficient home ... she created a very happy ship.'

'I am sorry,' Webster offered. 'That is tragic.'

'Thank you, but life has to go on and I think of her as lucky dead, rather than dead lucky.'

'Yes,' Yellich spoke softly. 'I know what you mean.'

'Do you?'

'Yes, I think I do. We see life ... police officers see life, it's the nature of the beast ... and I think I fear permanent severe disability more than I fear death. As you say, sir, there has to be a certain quality of life, a certain minimum quality to make life bearable.'

'Yes,' Tony Rigall smiled, 'that's a very good way of putting it. So there was, overnight, a huge gap in the house and it was shortly after that occurring that that woman arrived. That damned Canadian. No one could have replaced Amelia ... no one ... and I didn't want to replace her on an emotional level, no one could have done that, as I said, but I did need someone to organize the house. We ... I had a cook ... I didn't want her to cook in the kitchen and we had maids to clean, so I advertised for ... for I don't know what ... a house manager, someone to run the place on a day-to-day basis in the way my lovely wife had done. Someone to keep the overview.' Rigall leaned back in his chair and glanced upwards. 'Big mistake ... that was the story of Julia arriving ... she had no references but no one else wanted the job and she impressed well at the interview.'

'Where did she come from? Did she say?' Yellich glanced upwards at the ornate ceiling.

'Canada. She was newly arrived from Canada. She said that she was looking for a new start in life.' Rigall drew heavily on the cigarette. 'She seemed to settle in, seemed to be pleasant at first. Then our cook left without saying why she was leaving, and then the maids. I knew the maids would leave when cook left because the maids were ... well, I don't want to sound patronizing but by means of explanation I'll describe them as "simple-minded", and cook kept an eye on them. She was very protective towards them, motherly almost. She wouldn't let anyone put upon them ... but cook leaving was a shock, cook was really in with the bricks. It turned out that the Canadian female just irritated her; she just wouldn't stay out of the kitchen, always interfering. In any house of this size the kitchen belongs to the cook and if you don't know that, or don't accept that, then you are in trouble. That's the rule. It's the cook's kitchen. That's it. So, it came to the point that cook had just had enough; she took off her apron, left it on the kitchen table and cycled home, never to return. The maids followed her. At that time I was out of the house most of the day attending to business. I never saw any of the friction developing, and eventually it was the head gardener who tipped me off. "I'd be off as well", he said, "but I'm in the garden all day and I have my hut to go to when it's wet, so I am away from the house, away from the Canadian female".'

'I see.'

'So I let her go. I let the Canadian female go. I had to. Wretched woman. I gave her a reference that would get her started somewhere else, so that was unfair of me but I wasn't inclined to defend a case for unfair dismissal in the county court. That could have been very costly.'

Yellich and Webster remained silent. Webster, who with Yellich had visited the Canadian woman's next employer in his stone cold home, thought that 'unfair' did not adequately describe Rigall's act of dumping his troubles on another unsuspecting person as a means of solving said troubles. Edith Hemmings, as she became, had left Rigall's household to work for Alexander Beattie and whilst there had emptied the elderly man's bank account and stolen his meagre possessions. 'Unfair' just wasn't the word, thought Webster, just not the word at all. Then Rigall said something which made Webster's attitude towards him soften.

'Only when she had gone did I realize what she had done,' he explained. 'I gave her access to the money to buy food and fuel and found out later that the account had been cleared out. Not all my money ... that is separate and safe ... but the money I put into the account to run the house. The household budget account. Then I found out she had stolen my wife's jewellery. I called the police but we didn't know where she had gone; the cheques she had written were made out to cash. The jewels would have been sold for hard cash. I have now replaced my domestic staff and have appointed Lionel, the butler who opened the door to you, and he costs an arm and a leg. But the sense of loss remains.'

'So what sort of woman was Julia, apart from being dishonest? Apart from rubbing people up the wrong way?' Yellich asked.

Rigall smiled. 'Well, what else can there be after that?' He paused. 'But I really can't answer your question, she never let me get close to her, and I never wanted to, and so any conversation we had was always short and to the point.'

'Did she tell you much about herself? Her background?'

'No ... no ... she didn't. She was quite

private in that sense, quite a private person. She was recently arrived from Canada, that I did find out, but she never spoke about her family. She came from Quebec province, I believe, she did tell me that and also that she then moved to Ontario ... lived near Toronto for a while, just before coming to the UK.'

'Would you say she was hiding, or running from something?'

'Yes ... yes,' Rigall smiled briefly and nodded. 'You know you could say that, yes, you could. In fact, come to think of it, someone did come to look for her. A Canadian man – it's all coming back now. I was a man obsessed with the theft of my money and of my wife's jewellery and with the driving away of excellent staff ... but yes, she was a person in hiding. She had strange hiding away habits now that you mention it ... stayed indoors, in the house and the garden. She'd walk in the rear garden to take the air but never the front. Very infrequently she'd leave the house, just once a week perhaps, even once every two weeks, to buy provisions and cash cheques and sell Amelia's jewellery. So, yes, in hiding, a woman in hiding. A very unpleasant character, and I am so pleased she has gone ... it was a big mistake to hire her. So why all the interest?'

'She was murdered,' Yellich explained, in a matter-of-fact tone of voice.

'Now why doesn't that surprise me?' Rigall leaned forward and, resting his elbows on his knees, shook his head slowly. 'Why doesn't that surprise me at all? I can understand that, I can really understand why someone would want to do her in. When was this?'

'Recently, a few days ago.'

'Where?'

'Not too far from here.'

'There's been no mention of it in the media ... that's something I would have noticed.'

'We decided on a news blackout ... for now.'

'I see.' Rigall reclined in his chair. 'Murdered you say? Well, well, well ... why am I not at all surprised...?'

'Tell us more about the Canadian.'

'The man you mean ... the man who came looking for her?'

'Yes, that man.'

Rigall paused. 'He came very recently ... a few months ago. He was on her trail though, he had her scent.'

'What did he want ... do you know? Did he say?'

'Her ... madam. He wanted her. I told him that she had left two years ago but that didn't seem to disappoint him, in fact he smiled and said, "Getting closer. I am getting closer".'

'He came here?'

'Yes. Walked up to the door and knocked on it. He was as bold as brass and as calm as you please. He spoke to Lionel who was unsure of him and asked him to wait outside ... it was a little cold that day but Lionel did the right thing. He is very good like that. He came to find me ... I was in here, in this very room, and so I went to the door and he was every inch a Canadian. To look at him you'd think "lumberjack", broad-chested, powerfully built, trimmed dark beard, patterned jacket and a fur hat, a man's fur hat ... you know the type.'

'Yes ... yes.'

'He asked for Julia Avrillé. It was then I told him she had left a few years ago. He asked where she had gone and I told him I didn't know but I believed she had remained in the vicinity ... she was somewhere in the Vale of York.'

'How did you know that?'

'I saw her, saw her a few times driving an old car. It was the car that caught my eye, a mid 1960s saloon, a Wolseley or a Riley, white with a red flash down the side, a real classic. Lovely car. It's the only one of its kind hereabouts, damn few left in all England and that is the only one in the Vale, of that I am certain. I have an interest in classic cars you see. So she drove past and then I saw it was her at the wheel, wearing her wig but it was her. Did I mention she always wore a wig when she went out?'

'It's all right, we know about the wig.'

'Very well. The Canadian hung around for a few days, and unlike his quarry he made no attempt to hide himself. He seemed to base himself in Malton ... that was his operational base. He became a bit of a local figure and he liked his English beer, which is strange for a Canadian or an American. When they are over here they seem to prefer lager because that is very similar to American beer ... served chilled like American beer ... and the same colour, but English beer, brown coloured and served at room temperature, is not to their taste. You know I once saw a group of American sailors, first time in the UK, that was obvious, they came into a pub and ordered beer. The way they looked at it, absolutely aghast, then the way their faces screwed up when they tasted it ... it really was so very funny. Anyway, someone in the pub realized what had happened and told them that he'd been in the States and knew how they liked their beer to be served and he suggested that they try the lager, which they did and were very happy campers after that ... but the Canadian ... he liked his English beer. He had acquired the taste. So the point being that a publican in Malton might remember him.'

'You'll be the police?' The man leaned against the back of the bar of the Jolly Waggoner in Malton, dressed in a neatly pressed white shirt and black trousers with a black clip-on tie. He wiped a glass with a starched white towel. 'You have just visited Mr Rigall, the fox hunting man.'

'He hunts?' Yellich replied, observing a clean and neatly kept pub.

'Rides to hounds is the correct term but yes, he hunts the fox in his hunting pink and white breeches and black hat. He has some status in the hunt. He's not the master but has some significant position. He is a very and a most proper gentleman, is the good Mr Rigall.'

Webster and Yellich noticed a note of sarcasm in the publican's voice.

'You don't like the hunt?' Webster probed.

The barman shrugged, 'I wouldn't protest against it, but I wouldn't protest for it. I dare say I am what is known as a camp follower. I support the hunt without being part of it.'

'Interesting position to put yourself in,' Yellich smiled.

'Well, this is rural England. It's about as rural as it can get and in here you pick up the local attitude and the local attitude is "leave the hunt alone". I am not local myself. I came down from "the boro", but I have to make this pub work.'

'The "boro"?'

'Middlesbrough, Teesside ... which is about as urban and industrial as you can get.'

'Ah...'

'Well, folk round here haven't a good word

to say for the fox, it's an "animal of an animal" they say. If the fox just took what it needed it wouldn't be so bad but you see I am told that if a fox gets into a chicken run and there are twenty chickens in the run, it will kill all of them, then make its way home taking just the one chicken it needs to feed himself and his litter. But you see, for some smallholders and agricultural labourers, the loss of all their chickens to wantonness is a lot to bear ... it's a big loss for them. No fresh eggs ... no poultry ... have to buy it all until they can restock with more chickens.'

'I can imagine.'

'And the hunt also brings in big money and keeps traditional rural crafts alive. We have a blacksmith and he's only here because the hunt keeps him in work. He can walk down the main street holding his head up as a proud man but without the hunt he'd be nothing ... a man on the dole, looking for work, any work, no matter how menial.'

'Interesting point of view.'

'So I say, keep the hunt, it keeps the money coming in and we need it, trade is slow but we are still afloat.'

Webster glanced round the pub. A few

elderly men, four he counted, sitting silently, apart from each other and in front of glasses of beer. Slow trade as the publican said, but, Webster pondered, he is at least still open midweek which is more than the lot of the publican of The Hunter's Moon in Stillington.

'So how can I help you, gentlemen?'

'Yes, we have visited Mr Rigall...'

'One of his estate workers drinks in here,' the publican smiled. 'Called in for one on his way home for his lunch, he is a bit of a daytime drinker but he can handle it, and he told me to expect you.'

'Yes, he was correct to tell you to expect us. We are looking for a Canadian gentleman; we believe he might have been in here enjoying a beer, some months ago now.'

'Piers?' The publican smiled broadly. 'Piers, the Canadian?'

'Is that Piers?' Webster showed the computer E-FIT to the publican.

'Yes ... well, it could be Piers, there is a likeness, Piers was the only Canadian to hang round here. Went away, then came back to see us a few days ago ... nice bloke, he said he had done what he came to do ... job done, he said. He looked more satisfied than pleased; he said he was shortly to be going back to Canada. He bought a beer and put one in the pump for me. We shook hands and he walked out the door ... and that's the last I saw of him.'

'A few days ago?' Yellich could not conceal his excitement.

'Yes, Tuesday of this week, day before yesterday. It would be mid evening when he called in, seven, eight p.m., that sort of time. He used to stay with Mrs Stand.'

'Mrs Stand?'

'Next door but one ... that way,' the publican pointed to his left. 'Double fronted house, Broomfield Hotel to give it its proper name, but it's a guest house ... bed and breakfast, not a proper hotel. He stayed there.'

Yellich smiled. 'Thanks,' he said. 'Thanks a lot.'

George Hennessey spent that morning at his desk addressing necessary paperwork. He was all too aware of the gripes of police officers about the mountain of forms they have to complete and reports they have to write, but he found that he enjoyed paperwork and he gave a lot of care to the task, knowing as he did the necessity of accurate and up-to-the-minute recording. At midday, and noticing the sleet-laden rain had eased, although the cloud cover remained at ten tenths in RAF speak, he stood and clambered into his woollen coat, wound a scarf round his neck and screwed his brown fedora on his head. He walked casually from his office and signed as being 'out' at the front desk and, after exchanging a word with the cheery police constable who was on duty there, he stepped out of the building into a grimy Micklegate Bar. He glanced up, as he often did, drawn with horrific fascination, at the spikes on the wall above the arch where the heads of traitors to the Crown were impaled and then left for three years as a warning to any other would-be renegade, the last such impaling taking place during the mid eighteenth century. Hennessey crossed the road and climbed the steps on to the wall and turned to his right to walk the wall from the Bar to Baile Hill, knowing, as every York resident knows, that walking the walls is by far the speediest and most efficient means of crossing the city. The stretch of wall he walked that day was, he always found, the most pleasing, affording good views of the neat and desirable terraced houses of Lower Priory Street and Fairfax and Hampden Streets which stood snugly and smugly 'within the walls', and to his right the much less expensive, the less desirable, less cared-for houses of the streets joining Nunnery Lane, being 'without the walls'. The last few feet of that stretch of wall ended in a small copse which Hennessey always thought had a certain mystical quality about it. He left the wall at Baile Hill, as indeed he had to, and crossed the road bridge over the cold and deceptively sluggish looking River Ouse, turning right on to Tower Street and, exploiting an infrequent gap in the traffic, jogged hurriedly across the road. Once over the River Foss at Castle Mills Bridge, he was, as he always thought, in 'any town – UK'.

It was an area of small terraced housing with inexpensive cars parked at the kerb. He glimpsed a motorcycle chained to a lamp post, the unexpected sight of which caused a shaft of pain to pierce his chest. He continued, walking up quiet Hope Street, crossing Walmgate and entering Navigation Road. He was by then deeply within the part of the city which could have been anywhere in England. All round him were the same type of small terraced houses with only the light grey colour of the brick suggesting that he was in the Vale of York. Hennessey strolled on and turned into Speculation Street and at the end of the street he walked through the low doorway of The Speculation Inn. He turned immediately to his left and entered the taproom. In the corner, on the hard bench which ran round the corner of the room, in front of a small circular table, sat a slightly built, smartly dressed middle-aged man. The man smiled at Hennessey; Hennessey nodded to the man and walked to the serving hatch, there being no bar in the taproom of The Speculation. Hennessey bought a whisky and soda and a glass of tonic water with lime from the jovial young woman who served him. He carried the drinks across to where the middle-aged man sat and he placed the whisky in front of him. Hennessey then sat on a highly polished stool in front of the man and raised the glass of tonic water,

'Your health, Shored-Up.'

'And yours, Mr Hennessey. And yours.' The man eagerly sipped the whisky. 'You come to your humble and obedient servant this day as a ray of sunshine would come upon a dark place. I didn't know how I was going to make that drink last and then you walked in the door ... a saviour to a man in need.'

'Well, I may have need of you ... anyway I see you survived Her Majesty's Prison, Shored-Up?'

'Oh, Mr Hennessey, I tell you, HM hotels are getting rougher and rougher. So very rough. I had to share a cell with three others, and our cell was originally a cell designed for one, and they were all rough boys ... that terrible youth...' The man shuddered. 'How I resent him.'

'The one that dobbed you in?'

'Yes, him ... that one ... who dobbed me in, as you say. No sense of honour.'

'You would have done the same, Shored-Up, especially if it meant avoiding a spell inside ... which is what he avoided.'

'How is a man to make a decent living? The dole goes nowhere. It wouldn't keep a church mouse alive … and I never harmed anyone … I don't do violence.'

'Stealing elderly ladies' Rolls Royces…'

'Yes, but not harming the ladies themselves and so lucrative … a way of making a living.'

'So criminal also.' Hennessey cast an eye over the man's clothing. Expensive at first glance, threadbare at the second and as always saying 'charity shops' very loudly at the third glance. The image of the 'distressed gentleman' came to Hennessey's mind, usefully assisted by the man's 'gentlemanly' manner, which had been honed over the years by observing the real thing. 'So are you at it again?'

The man shrugged. He delicately sipped the whisky Hennessey had bought him. 'Chap has to earn his living … there are no free rides.'

'You've been out how long? Can't be a full month yet?'

'Three weeks tomorrow.' The man smiled, 'I confess that fresh air never did taste so sweet. Now I am settling into my nice new flat. I gave up the old one; or rather it gave up on me.'

'Yes, I can imagine you'd have difficulty

161

paying rent when you're inside doing twelve to the inch.'

'I had a little put by. I could have kept the flat going but paying rent on an empty flat, it went so much against the grain. Flats are easy to come by, and I quite like my new little drum. And I escaped the torture of sewing mailbags, opted for education, "good citizenship" in the main. Easier and anyway they don't sew mailbags in the prisons any more. The GC class enabled me to sit and daydream; usually I carried myself off to a sun drenched and very faraway place.'

'And now you are seeking another victim?' Hennessey growled.

'Client, Mr Hennessey, please. They are your humble servant's clients.'

'Clients,' Hennessey sighed, 'you mean a string of wealthy old ladies who seek male company of the manner that used to be enjoyed by them.'

'Provide comfort and succour to those in need ... that's what I do, Mr Hennessey.'

'Living and dining with ladies who pick up the bill.'

'And where is the crime in that, Mr Hennessey?'

'None, none at all, not until you begin to tell them about the tin mine in Bolivia which could produce unheard-of riches and which needs some development money to get it into full production or the location of the treasure-laden ship which went down in a storm some centuries ago ... and would they like to invest in a little mining concern or a salvage venture with a guarantee of their money back plus at least fifty per cent? It's then it becomes off side, very left field.'

'But I am also of use to you, Mr Hennessey, am I not? ... great use.'

'Which is why I am here.' Hennessey glanced up at the frosted windows upon which was etched the legend 'Sanders and Penn's Fine Ales', being a relic of the earlier days of The Speculation Inn when there was evidently a local brewery called 'Sanders and Penn'.

'Ah...' the man smiled. He drained his glass and pushed it across the highly polished, brass-topped table towards Hennessey.

'Not so fast. Two nights ago a woman was found by the side of the canal...'

'I know,' the man smiled.

'You know? How? We haven't released a

press statement.'

'Can't keep a thing like that quiet, it's not possible. The boys know, the boys in "the Den"; they know. Suspicious circumstances, the old jungle telegraph, the boys in the Den need to know things like that ... got to keep abreast of developments. Survival depends upon it.'

Hennessey sighed. 'I imagine, but the reason why I have called here in the hope of finding you "at home", as it were, is because the deceased, the victim, was not as clean as the driven snow herself, so we are discovering, quite a naughty lady. In fact you two would have made a very good team, you fleecing old ladies and she fleecing her gentlemen employers. What a duo you would have made.'

'Really?' There was a glint in the man's eyes. 'Now you tell me.'

'She was a Canadian.'

'Not Becky?' Shored-Up looked genuinely saddened. 'You don't mean Becky?'

'You know her?'

'Becky the Canadian, black hair but liked to wear a blonde wig?'

'Yes, sounds like her,' Hennessey groaned,

164

'and Becky is yet another alias, Julia and Edith being two others. Doubtless there will be more.'

'Well, this is a small town, Mr Hennessey, and the brothers and sisters all know each other ... she gave her name as Becky Lecointe.'

Hennessey stood and walked to the serving hatch. He returned with another whisky and placed it in front of the man and said, 'So, tell me what you know about Becky Lecointe.'

'Well, she got to know the boys and girls in the Den.'

'Being the taproom of The Mitre in Blossom Street?'

'Might be...' The man picked up the glass of whisky and savoured the bouquet.

'It is ... but carry on.'

'Well, it explains why I drink in here at lunchtimes. I have to be discreet, you understand. It's a long way from Blossom Street in York terms, and it also explains why sometimes I insist on meeting your good self out of town.'

'I remember,' Hennessey growled. 'I can't decide whether or not my abiding dislike for

Rotherham is greater than my abiding dis-like for Doncaster ... but thank you for intro-ducing me to both towns. My life is enriched by the experiences of visiting both.'

'Please,' the man sipped his drink lovingly, 'but it is necessary to be discreet, as I said. I play a dangerous game, Mr Hennessey, it's part of the thrill and while we all will meet our maker I do not wish to bring that unique event upon me any sooner than I have to.'

'That I can understand,' and again pain ran deep within Hennessey's chest, two shafts, one for Jennifer and one for Graham. 'So ... in your own words...'

'The Canadian ... thief.'

'Yes.'

'Selling jewellery she'd half inched. She got a better price for it in the Den than in the pawnbrokers. Folk only do that if it's half inched. If it's theirs and they want it back then they pawn it. But she was interested only in getting all the cash she could. So it was pinched. Also a few wallets.'

'She dipped?'

'Oh yes ... a woman's touch you under-stand, more adept at getting inside a man's inside pocket.'

'Strange we never got to know her ... she must have been good ... in a criminal sense of the word.'

'The Canadian police do.'

'Do they?'

'So she said. She was anxious to return to Canada, she was unhappy in the UK. Me, I wouldn't want to live anywhere but the UK, dare say she feels the same way about Canada, or felt the same, I should say. Home being home ... wherever the heart is an' all that stuff.'

'Yes.' Hennessey glanced up at the frosted glass of The Speculation Inn. Through the areas of clear glass he saw dark clouds looming ominously and rapidly.

'So she told us she was waiting until the heat died down before going back; it seems that for her it was a case of any port in a storm.'

'I see.' Hennessey sipped a little of his drink. 'Strange she found The Mitre.'

'She was in the area for a good few months before she found us, but like always finds like. If you hang around any city long enough you'll find your own kind. Story was that she needed a fence, someone to take the stolen stuff off her, and eventually she found The Mitre. She really was in a good way of business. She even turned windows. Very unusual for a woman, and a woman of her years as well.'

'Turned windows!'

'Yes, she was a most adept burglar. Most adept. Or she could con and would con and charm her way into an old person's house. She had a calm manner and a ready smile. She also had an ID card.'

'Of?'

'A social worker. She had dipped a social worker, found his ID in his wallet and realizing its usefulness she had kept it. The photo was a clean shaven, dark-haired young male, but it was all that was needed to con a partially sighted elderly person desperate for company, as so many of them are. So she would get into the elderly person's house, leave with something of value and unload it in the Den. She wanted cash ... only cash, as we all do. Wouldn't take it to a jeweller who'd be suspicious, and they have CCTV in their shops. So it was either the Den or the pawnbroker but she preferred the Den. If she couldn't sell it in the Den only then would she pawn it. I used to feel sorry for her husband, poor soul.'

'Oh...' Hennessey sipped his tonic water. 'Why?'

'Well, he's thinking he's got a nice wife to come home to and all the while she's roaming the Vale ... and out to the coast.'

'The coast?'

'Oh yes, where do you go when you retire but the coast? Lots of easy pickings on the coast.' He sipped his whisky.

'She was doing this recently?'

'Last week. She did a house last week somewhere and had got herself a bag of gold and ice. It was all worth thousands but she sold it for hundreds.'

'Some woman,' Hennessey shook his head. 'We think someone was looking for her. Do you know anything about that?'

'Yes,' the man leaned forwards, 'she was a frightened woman. Someone was on her trail, hunting her, and she was frightened of him. The wig, you see, an attempt at disguise. She'd take it off in the Den but put it on when it was time to leave.'

'Did she drink?'

'No, well always only fruit juice. Never

169

touched booze. Playing safe. Can't be the dutiful wife, his to come home to, with breath smelling of booze.'

'Astounding.'

'Not a nice woman at all. Couldn't trust her, even among thieves. It doesn't surprise me at all that someone offed her. Does not surprise me at all. Not in the slightest.'

'Doesn't surprise me either.' Hennessey glanced round the room, the hard bench which stood against the wall, the circular brass-topped tables with stools around them, low ceiling, no decoration at all, hardwearing floor surface. The Speculation had not ever been modernized, as if, it seemed to Hennessey, it was waiting to be discovered by the real ale real pub brigade. 'Just who was she?'

The man shrugged and smiled and pushed his glass across the shiny brass surface of the table, holding a pleading manner of eye contact with Hennessey as he did so.

'No more for you, Shored-Up, not from my pocket, but if you get a line on the fella that was looking for her, then contact me. If it's good news you'll get a serious wedge.'

'And perhaps also a good word in for me

with my probation officer, Miss Pratt? Oh my ... a tyrant ... what with her and the youth who informed on me ... my life is a trifle difficult at the moment.'

'Maybe. The fella who was looking for Becky is also a Canadian, well built, chequered or tartan jacket, beard, fur hat, likes British beer. Strange that, stalking someone to kill them but finding time to enjoy the local beer as though he was on holiday.' Hennessey stood. 'But do try and get by on the dole. No more Lt Colonel Smythe (retired) of the Devon and Dorsets, or you'll be back in the slammer. And you know how much you like all those rough boys.'

'Too late for me to learn new skills, Mr H, far too late, I'm an old dog now.'

'And keep your appointments with Miss Pratt.'

'She's a tyrant, still only in her twenties and a tyrant already.'

'That,' Hennessey buttoned his coat, 'sounds exactly like the probation officer you need.'

The owner of the Broomfield Hotel smiled a warm, wide smile and opened the booking ledger. She was a small framed woman, dressed in a business suit and giving off a soft aroma of perfume. 'Two rooms, gentlemen?'

'No rooms,' Yellich showed his ID. 'Sorry,' he added with a smile.

He thought the woman's smile in response was forced. Business could not be good for the Broomfield Hotel, Malton. 'Sorry to disappoint you.'

'Well, it is a seasonal sort of business, winter is always a low time and this winter seems to be hanging on, quite reluctant to go. We get a few businessmen in the winter, that carries us through, or folk staying here while they are looking up relatives. So how can I help you?' Mrs Stand continued to smile warmly.

'We were told you recently put up a Canadian gentleman, tall man, beard, chequered or tartan jacket, seemed to like local beer. Quite recently ... a matter of days ago.'

'Yes ... yes, we did. What would you like to know about him?'

'All you can tell us.'

The dining room of the Broomfield Hotel was, said the proprietor, 'as good a place as any to talk' and she escorted them there. The room had ten tables; all the tables had white cloths and cutlery lay neatly in wooden trays upon a sideboard. The room smelled of furniture polish and air freshener. The world passed the room on the other side of net curtains.

'Well, he came,' said the woman as she and the officers sat at one of the larger tables. 'His name ... can't recall his last name but his first name was Piers ... he liked to be called Piers.'

'Yes, the publican gave that name.'

'He paid cash as I recall, so never any cheque or credit card, so I never found out his surname. Doubt if I would remember it if I did ... my memory ... it was never good and now it's getting worse.'

'You remember his Christian name though,' Yellich spoke softly.

'Only because Piers is a name that has personal significance for me. It's my brother's name.'

'I see. So what sort, what manner of man was he?'

'Well I remember he had a warm manner but his mind was focused. He was not here on holiday. He was one of those guests who stay here because he had a task to fulfil. He came here a few times over the years. First time must have been about two years ago ... last time was a few days ago, as you said. If you are in this business you remember the good guests and you remember the bad guests and you remember the regulars. You also get a feel for guests. I grew up in a guest house in the Lake District so I have been in this game one way or another all my life and you do get a feel ... and Piers was a man with a mission.'

'He never said what that mission was?' Yellich probed. 'No indication even?'

'No,' the proprietor shook her head, 'no, he played his cards close to his chest. Piers was a good guest, clean ... neat ... well spoken ... quiet ... reserved. He went out each morning and returned each evening with beer on his breath but his conduct was still perfect so he didn't drink a lot. He was always in by ten which is when I lock the door. I can't keep the door open all night like a big hotel can. I have a maid who helps but at night, in the evenings, I am by myself, I don't even have a dog. I can't retire for the night and leave the front door unlocked. That would be asking for trouble.'

'Of course,' Webster agreed, 'that would be unwise ... even in civilized Malton.'

'Do you know how he travelled about?' Yellich asked.

'Car.'

'You didn't get the registration number?' Yellich asked hopefully.

The proprietor shook her head and smiled sheepishly as if to say, 'sorry, no'.

'So when did he leave this last time?'

'See ... Thursday today, it would be Tuesday, Tuesday in the evening. Yes, my bridge night. I host a bridge school here each Tuesday and I remember that I had to leave the table to allow him to settle his bill ... so Tuesday. Definitely Tuesday, two evenings ago.'

'You will have cleaned his room by now?'

'Yes and re-let it but if you wish to inspect it to look for fingerprints or whatever, then please do so.'

'Thank you, we'll do that,' Yellich nodded. 'He might have left us a print on an obscure surface. Is the room being let out at the moment?'

'No, the guest who had that room left this

175

morning.'

'Well, if you could keep it empty, the SOCO boys will be here tomorrow.'

'SOCO?'

'Scene of Crime Officers.'

'Ah ... but yes, of course. I am quiet at the moment, as you have seen ... no problem about keeping one room un-let.'

'Thank you. He didn't leave any item, any possession behind him?'

'No, sorry, he didn't. Some guests leave their room looking like one large dustbin; just leave anything they don't want and leave it anywhere they wish, floor ... on the bed ... anywhere, but Piers, he picked up after himself. He was one of the good guests. I could do with more like him.'

'I see. Did he ever ask directions or seek local knowledge or any other information?' Yellich asked.

'No ... no ... Piers was very independent, very self-reliant. He did have a road map of the area, I saw him looking very studiously at it over breakfast one morning. But he never asked directions or where anything was, he was just the quiet Canadian who only spoke if he was spoken to. Quiet but also with a purpose, who cleaned up his room after him, paid in cash, and left.'

Hennessey grunted in response to the gentle and reverent tap on his office door. He glanced up and saw Carmen Pharoah standing at the door frame. He thought she looked worried. He said so.

'Yes, sir,' Carmen Pharoah entered the room and stood in front of Hennessey's desk. She held a piece of paper in her hand. 'I have contacted the Canadians, sir, to notify them of the death of Edith Hemmings née Avrillé, just to note them of her death; it is really up to her husband to notify the next of kin.'

'Yes.'

'But...' she sank unbidden on to the chair in front of Hennessey's desk, 'there is a lot more to this...'

'As we are finding out.' Hennessey put down his pen with clear resignation and sat back in his chair. 'Go on, tell me.'

'Well, the upshot is that she is known to the Canadian police ... Edith Avrillé, date of birth ... place of birth ... same woman ... also known as Lecointe.'

'Oh, interesting.'

'Well, she was known to the Canadian authorities. Just petty stuff a long time ago.'

'Was?' Hennessey's eyebrows closed, his brow furrowed.

'She died three years ago,' Carmen Pharoah explained calmly. 'Whoever it is who's in the metal drawer at York District Hospital, it is not Edith Avrillé.'

Reginald Webster drove home, taking the quieter, more picturesque B1222 from York via Stillingfleet and Cawood to Selby. He drove up to his house and pumped the horn twice followed by a single third blast ... one-two ... pause ... three. It was the long agreed signal between himself and Joyce. If the neighbours didn't like it, none of them complained and he only ever used the signal during the day or early evening. Never at night when his neighbours would be abed. As he left the car, Joyce opened the door and smiled in his direction and allowed herself to be pushed aside by Terry as he darted out of the house to greet Webster. Webster walked up to the house with Terry and embraced his wife and she responded warmly and they closed the door behind the three of them.

Webster made the supper that evening, as was usual in the winter months, while his wife ran her fingers over the Braille book she was currently reading. She longed to cook for her husband but he was adamant, it was just far, far too dangerous for her to work with heat and boiling water. In the summer a well prepared salad was most welcome for him to come home to but in the winter, when hot food was needed, then he did the cooking, and did so at his insistence.

That evening he took Terry for his walk. The long-haired Alsatian was a happy dog, as are all dogs who have jobs to do, but guiding Joyce throughout the day was no substitute for exercise, and he needed his 'off duty' time to wander and explore the dense woodland close to where the Websters lived. Reginald Webster watched the lithe and placid dog as he wound his way in and out of the frost-covered landscape and again marvelled at his wife's courage, facing her blindness with such stoicism. All the worse because at the time of the accident she had been studying fine art at university. She thought herself fortunate because, of the four people in the car that night, it was only she who had survived.

Humble.

Again, his wife made him feel very, very humble.

Thomson Ventnor drove home and changed into a lightweight Italian suit and a white overcoat. He took a bus to the outskirts of York and walked slowly up a long driveway to a large nineteenth century house and opened the front door. He was met with a blast of excessively warm air which he always thought could not possibly be healthy. He signed in the visitor book and climbed a wide, deeply carpeted stairway and entered a room in which a number of people sat, all still and quiet, apparently not interacting with each other at all. In one corner of the room a young woman gently moved an electric razor over the face of an elderly man. She and Ventnor nodded and smiled at each other. Another elderly man, seated in the opposite corner, grinned in recognition of Ventnor, but by the time Ventnor reached him, the man had retreated somewhere within his mind and all Ventnor could do was to sit beside him and say, 'Hello, dad.'

Having stayed at the home for half an hour and talked to the staff about his father's wellbeing, Ventnor left the building and took a bus into York. He wandered from pub to pub having a pint of beer in each and eventually fetched up at Caesar's Night Club. He got into conversation with a woman who had forced herself into a dress that was too small and too short for her and had a trying-hard-to-be-nice smile. He thought she had the worn look of a retired lady of the night, or perhaps of someone trying to put something unpleasant behind her, but it was at least female company and she seemed interested in him. When the closing lights came on she said, 'See you around?'

'Yes,' Ventnor replied, holding eye contact with her. 'Don't know when. I'm going to Canada tomorrow, don't know when I'll be back … it's an open-ended trip.'

'Well, that's a new one,' she snorted as she grabbed her handbag and twisted off the bar stool to begin, on unsteady legs, to walk across the floor towards the exit sign.

'It happens to be true', he said to himself. 'Only found out myself a few hours ago'.

It was Friday, 02.00 hours.

FOUR

Saturday, 17.30 hours
*in which Yellich and Ventnor travel overseas and
the gentle reader is privy to the demons which
haunt Carmen Pharoah and also to those which
haunt George Hennessey.*

Yellich thought that Aiden McLeer did indeed look like a Canadian, whatever Canadians are supposed to look like. McLeer was
well built, broad chested, muscular, neatly
dressed in a grey suit with a red tie over a
white shirt. He was short-haired, but not
crew cut, and was clean shaven. He had an
air of affability about him, Yellich found,
which mixed wholesomely with an attitude
of politeness, humility and gentleness. He
had a slow but very masculine way of moving and Yellich thought that had he not been

an officer in the Barrie Police Homicide Unit, he would have been clad in fur, trapping for beaver in the vast, snow covered wilderness. McLeer, Yellich and Ventnor sat in McLeer's office in the Barrie Police headquarters on Sperling Drive, Cundles East, Barrie, which had transpired to be a newly built building of brick walls with vast window areas, under a pale green painted roof of metal sheeting. The flagpoles stood in a small traffic island in front of the building; the one to the left had a flag flying the red maple leaf of Canada, the second, the emblem of the Barrie Police. McLeer's office, air-conditioned, at the front of the building, looked out over the rear of a large Zehrs shopping mall that Yellich and Ventnor were to find was pronounced 'z-hears'. The rest of the police station was bounded by Highway 400 from which came the constant hum of car tyres rotating at speed over the road surface.

'I read over the report your boss faxed to us yesterday. It made very interesting reading. Our chief has asked me to head up at our end.' McLeer had a soft speaking voice with a distinct Canadian accent. He was not a migrant, definitely first, second or even third generation Canadian, possibly more. He was, Yellich immediately found, a man who seemed to be at peace in his own country.

'Yes, sir,' Yellich responded quickly. He felt a little on edge, he felt eager and keen to make a good, and also a lastingly good, impression amongst the Canadians.

'Aiden, please,' McLeer smiled at him. His eyes were warm, sincere, blue.

'Thank you. I am Somerled,' Yellich replied, 'S.O.M.E.R.L.E.D., pronounced "Sorley". It's Celtic, quite old I believe.'

'I was going to ask,' McLeer grinned. 'It's a name I have never come across before.'

Thomson Ventnor added, 'Dare say you'll find that I have another strange name.'

'I do.' Again a warm smile.

'It's also unusual, but it's only a north of England variation of Thomas. I am the third Thomson Ventnor.'

'Interesting.'

'You grow up with an unusual name,' Yellich explained, 'and after a short while it just becomes ... well, ordinary. You do learn to live with it getting remarked upon each time you meet someone new, but that's easily coped with.'

'I can imagine.' McLeer clawed his mug of coffee in a meaty paw and added, 'I thought Aiden was a little unusual, but as you say, after a while ... Well, the report ... we can talk about unusual names later.'

'Yes,' Yellich sat forward, 'dare say we'd better get down to business.'

'Indeed, well the report seems clear enough.' Aiden McLeer held the fax in his left hand. 'A lady who is ... who was not who she claimed to be and who was murdered, possibly by a Canadian male who travelled to England for the express purpose of said murder. She further seems to have taken the identity of a Canadian lady who once lived in the city. Seems about it?'

'Yes, sir.'

'The Canadian link, the Canadian connection is clear ... the Barrie connection is clear ... and you have no local suspects?'

'None, sir ... sorry, Aiden. None, Aiden. She didn't seem to be particularly integrated in the legitimate community apart from her socially isolated marriage, but our boss, Mr Hennessey, has unearthed information that she was well submerged in the criminal milieu of York.'

'Yes, he said so ... to the complete ignorance of her husband.'

'Yes, sir, she is, she was, a lady who led multiple lives. She seemed to be trying to disprove the notion that you "can't be all things to all men".' Yellich sipped his coffee but yearned for tea. 'Her husband knew her only as a suburban housewife, keeping house for him. Yet when she did leave the house alone, she went out to engage in crime ... and she became known to the York underworld as "Becky".'

'How did her husband react to that news?'

'He didn't,' Yellich replied flatly. 'Or he hasn't yet.'

'You mean he doesn't know ... yet?'

'Yes, sir ... Aiden. "Yet" being the operative word. He'll learn of her true nature eventually but, at the moment, Mr Hennessey is leaving him alone with his grief and his mourning, an important process for him to go through. He needs time and space to go through it.'

'Yes, that is very thoughtful and very sensitive of your Mr Hennessey.'

'I think so,' Yellich smiled. 'I like working for him...'

'And there is also the issue of the Canadian man who was apparently stalking her ... and he is your prime suspect.'

'Well, looking for her, sir ... rather than stalking her.'

'Yes ... better, stalking means something else ... yes, and the implication is that he found her and left her on a canal bank to die of exposure. Cold winter you are having.'

'Unusually so, Aiden, confess this is warmer than we expected.'

McLeer glanced to his left out across the low-rise roof of Zehrs to the still bare trees and the blue sky beyond. 'Yes, seems spring is early this year, but don't get fooled. It will freeze tonight. That's why you can walk out in shirtsleeves right now but the lake is still iced over. When the sun goes down the temperature will drop like a stone. This warmth won't hang around; if you've brought your thermals with you, you'll need them this evening.'

'I see,' Yellich followed McLeer's gaze. The bare tree branches said it all for him. He was pleased he had indeed brought warm clothing. 'Small town,' Yellich observed. 'Seems so...'

'Yes, Barrie is quite small but,' McLeer smiled and shrugged his left shoulder, 'it's enough to keep us busy. Our buckets are full every Friday and Saturday night. So you have no local suspect for the murder of ... the lady in question?'

'None ... none at all, Aiden. All signs point to the Canadian gentleman who was trying to track her down. He paid cash wherever he went so as to avoid leaving a trail for us to follow and the photofit...'

'Yes,' McLeer picked up the photofit, 'square-jawed, bearded, no distinguishing features at all ... there's many like him in Barrie.'

'More's the pity.'

Ventnor glanced casually out of McLeer's office window and watched a young woman in jeans and a sweater push a young child in a buggy along the pavement beside Zehrs and he thought that he could be viewing a similar street scene in York, or indeed any-where in the UK, except that, when she crossed the road, the young woman looked left before looking right.

'Well,' McLeer sat back in his chair and interlaced the fingers of both hands behind his head. 'Not a lot to go on but we have solved cases with less to go on and we rise to the challenge. So, tell me, gentlemen, how's your French?'

'Non-existent,' Yellich admitted.

'Same here,' Ventnor added, with a distinct note of apology in his voice. 'Why?'

'Ah ... the English,' McLeer smiled a broad smile and released his fingers and placed his meaty hands gently on his desk, 'you expect everybody to speak English but you do not attempt to learn other languages. Not true, I know, but I have heard that said of the English many times.'

'We don't really have the incentive to be fair,' Yellich said defensively, 'English being the international language, especially of commerce and air travel.'

'Fair enough, but the reason I ask is the name, Piers ... Piers, you see, is French, and one of the names the deceased used was Edith Lecointe. Lecointe is French also. If I know Canada, if I know my country, I think we will be venturing into the French Canadian community. Mainly it is centred in

189

Ottawa and the rest of Quebec province but we have our fair share of French Canadians here in Ontario ... people ... families ... and I mean whole kinship groups for whom French is the language of choice. They are well integrated, they have not formed a ghetto or been forced into an enclave but they still form a distinct and separate group of citizens. Piers might well be an alias but the choice of Piers as a name would be a choice made by a French Canadian. Did he use a car when in the UK?'

'Yes, he did, we believe, a hire car, but no one took a note of the registration number,' Yellich explained. 'No one had any need to do so. And he wasn't caught on CCTV. Where he went was a bit remote for CCTV ... even in the UK.'

'And paid in cash. He was a man who clearly put a lot of effort into covering his tracks. I can see why you are suspicious of him.' McLeer paused. 'Seems to me we will need a French-speaking officer. I speak a little. It is expected of our officers to be as bilingual as possible but my French is not good enough if there is a possibility that we are going into the French Canadian community ... the French Canadians have developed their own form of French which makes French purists cringe.'

'I see,' Yellich said for want of something to say in reply. 'Interesting.'

'Not to worry, I have an officer in mind but she has authority in this matter, she has tactical command. This is a Barrie Police investigation. We must agree on that now.'

'That's understood,' Yellich nodded. 'And agreed.'

'Clear as a bell,' added Ventnor, 'protocol will be observed.'

'Cooperation will be of the fullest, of course, and we are keen to know how come Edith Lecointe's or Avrillé's name was used ... like, where is she now? There may be a heap more to this than the murder which occurred in England.'

'Absolutely, as is always the case.' Yellich raised his eyebrows and settled back in his chair. 'Yet the lady was frightened. She was scared of something or someone. She was in hiding, going out in disguise and doing what she could to raise hard cash and we don't know who she was, because neither her fingerprints nor her DNA are on our database.'

'None on ours either.' McLeer pronounced 'either' in the American way of 'ee-thuer' which grated on the ears of Yellich and Ventnor who both pronounced 'either' and 'neither' as 'I-ther' and 'ni-ther' as they had been taught and as they believed was the right and proper pronunciation. 'So,' McLeer continued, 'we have to find out who Edith Lecointe or Avrillé is ... or was.'

'It's the only place we can start,' Yellich offered.

'Yes, yes it is. How are you feeling?'

'Tired.' Yellich forced a grin.

'Yes, you would be.' McLeer looked at his watch. 'Four p.m ... .your body clock is at eight p.m., just a few hours' time difference at the moment. Usually it's five but we put our clocks forward two weeks before you do and back two weeks earlier also. So there are two two-week periods each year when we have a four-hour time difference, once in the spring and once in the fall but even so, four hours is still four hours and after a long flight. Is the hotel to your liking?'

'Yes, thank you.' It was, thought Yellich, a diplomatic reply.

'We put you centrally but you will find that it will be quiet. Barrie is not New York City, as you will see. Tomorrow I will introduce you to Sergeant Auphan, the French-speaking officer I have in mind. Sergeant Auphan has room at the moment to work with you on this case.'

'Thank you.' Yellich stood, as did Ventnor. Both men were weary and in need of a shower and a long sleep.

'So this is it ... this is where it all ended for little you ... little you and your little games.' The man looked at the area beyond the blue and white police tape which fluttered loudly in the strong breeze. '...All just to fetch up here ... and isn't it just such a lonely place to die? What a dance you led me ... what a dance, but I got you in the end, didn't I...? Eh...? Didn't I get you in the end?'

Sunday, 29th March, nine a.m.

The woman was tall, dark-haired, slender with high cheekbones. She had a gentleness of manner and a soft speaking voice which appealed to both Yellich and Ventnor. Particularly to Ventnor. She smiled warmly as she entered the room in which the two officers had been asked to wait, which overlooked the 400 Highway, the rooftops and thick stand of trees to the high-rise development of central Barrie in the mid distance. She extended her hand and said, 'Hello, I am Detective Sergeant Auphan, Marianne Auphan'. She slid gracefully behind the desk in the room and laid a manila folder on her highly polished desktop. She immediately invited Yellich and Ventnor to resume their seats with a deft feminine wrist action. 'So,' she said, 'Edith Lecointe.' She spoke with a slight French accent which suggested that was her dominant language although she was to prove herself word perfect in English. 'I have her file here. She died three years ago, aged forty-seven years. Is that in keeping with the age of the deceased in question?'

'Yes,' Yellich replied, 'it is.' He opened the file he carried and handed her photographs of the woman as she was found on the canal bank on the outskirts of York.

'Strange half sitting position,' Sergeant

Auphan remarked.

'Yes, we believe she was left for dead but in fact regained consciousness briefly only to succumb to hypothermia. The post-mortem revealed that she had no food in her stomach. We believe she was kept against her will for two days and deprived of food in that period. That of course didn't help her retain her body heat.'

'It wouldn't. A full stomach is like a form of central heating, or so we are constantly being told and in Canada it is vital to keep our young women eating sufficiently ... anorexia and Canadian winters are not a healthy combination, even if we or they do dress for it.' She turned and glanced out of her window. 'It's mild now but we will have more snow before the spring is finally here, then Ontario will bake. Believe me, gentlemen, in Ontario you are either in the fridge or in the oven with some in-between sort of days in spring and in the fall ... and they are few and far between.'

'So we believe,' Yellich answered.

'This is a fortunate time for you to come really, over the worst of winter and before the full force of summer. You might even find the weather tolerable. But, to the matter in hand, there is clearly foul play here,' she looked at the photographs, 'so our first port of call must be Edith Lecointe's last known address on Wattie Road in Midhurst. So, shall we go?'

Wattie Road, Midhurst revealed itself to be approximately two miles north of downtown Barrie. It was a narrow, winding road which both Yellich and Ventnor thought was poorly surfaced with cracks and potholes every few feet thus making driving a slow and careful procedure. The area itself was, it seemed, prestigious with large houses, some in the European style of two storeys with pronounced angled roofs, others in a more traditional New World style, a single storey but with a very broad frontage and with either a flat roof or a slightly angled roof, but all with a double garage built into or at the side of the main building, and each occupying its own very generous parcel of land. Each house also seemed to have a porch on which stood one or two plastic chairs, the observation of which triggered a distant memory of Yellich's of once reading that the favoured pastime of Canadians was sitting on the front porch in the long summer evenings. What few cars were parked in the driveways of the houses were new and large and mainly American, although catching sight of a solitary Jaguar made Ventnor feel at home. Between the houses and behind them were trees, at that time of year without foliage. What both the British officers noticed was how uniformly tall and upright the trees seemed, and how close together they stood, more akin to stalks in a cornfield than trees in a wood. So tightly packed were they that a man would have to weave continually between them if he were to make any progress through the woodland, and Yellich guessed that any man entering the wood and walking away from an observer on the roadside would be lost from sight ere he had walked ten feet. Yellich asked what sort of trees they were.

'Spruce,' Marianne Auphan replied confidently as she turned the unmarked car into the driveway of a wide, flat roofed property painted pale blue and halted the car between a bright yellow and highly polished Cherokee Jeep and a speedboat and trailer. 'They're green spruce, already.'

Marianne Auphan left the car and, without locking it, led Yellich and Ventnor to the house. She walked up the wooden steps of the porch and knocked on the door with an odd, thought Yellich, yet pleasing and effective mixture of reverence and authority, a knock which was clearly well rehearsed and practised. It was evident to both Yellich and Ventnor that Sergeant Auphan had honed her 'people skills' over the years and knew how to win the public over to her side. Her attitude made Yellich and Ventnor feel comfortable and wholly reassured. The door of the house opened and a middle-aged woman in a blue sweater and thick tartan patterned skirt stood in the doorway. She seemed to the officers to be well nourished; her figure may, they thought, be fairly described as 'curvy' but the 'curvy' nature seemed to have developed from a more slender figure of her youth. Her hair was silver and close cut. Spectacles hung on a silver chain round her neck as did not one, but three, necklaces. Her fingers were adorned with rings and stones. The wristwatch she wore was large and manly. 'Help you?' she asked, not seeming to be afraid of the strange woman and two strange men who had called on her without any prior warning.

Sergeant Auphan showed the householder her badge. 'Police,' she said softly. 'These two gentlemen are from the British Police.'

'The British Police!' The householder's voice was of a strange mixture of alarm that the police had called upon her, tinged with excitement and curiosity that two of the three officers were of the old country.

'Yes. Nothing for you to worry about,' Auphan spoke with a reassuring tone. 'I wonder if we can come in?'

'Sure.' The woman stepped aside and the officers entered and were met by two inquisitive cats, both grey and white and one noticeably larger than the other. Interlocking rubber matting had been placed over the carpet as a protective covering. The ceiling of the house seemed low to Yellich and Ventnor and the yellow and black pattern of the carpet which evoked a tiger skin was not to either man's taste. The house seemed unduly dark inside and rooms were separated by hanging fabric rather than doors, again not to the taste of either Yellich or Ventnor. 'I wasn't expecting no visitors,' the woman explained. 'It's a bit of a dumpster right about now.'

'Don't worry,' Auphan smiled gently, 'we are not from *Better Homes and Gardens*.'

'Well, come through.' The woman closed the front door behind the officers and led them to the rear of the house and invited them to sit at a circular table which was still covered with the manufacturer's plastic seal. The chairs were, the officers found, too low for the table and must have made eating from it somewhat difficult. To Yellich's right was a bookcase within which had been placed, oddly, he thought, a coffee making machine; to his left a window looked out across a rear garden which was still covered in a thick, but clearly thawing, layer of snow, and beyond the garden was yet another seemingly impenetrable stand of dark grey trunks of green spruce.

'We and the UK police,' Marianne Auphan began once the officers and the householder were seated round the circular table, 'are making inquiries into the late Edith Lecointe or Avrillé, once of this address.'

'Edith!' The woman gasped, her jaw slackened. 'Edith...'

'Yes.'

'She is gone before ... as you say, she is the late Edith Lecointe.'

'But this was her last address?'

'Yes. She and I lived here. She was my sister. I am Blanche Lecointe.'

'Well,' Marianne Auphan began, 'we need to know as much about your late sister as possible. I am sorry if this is difficult for you.'

'Difficult ... so sudden ... but why? Sorry ... I have to gather my thoughts...'

Marianne Auphan glanced at Yellich. 'Perhaps, Mr Yellich, you could explain?'

'Yes, of course.' Yellich sat forward and as he did so his eye was caught by a black squirrel sitting on the fence at the bottom of Blanche Lecointe's garden. He had not until then realized the subspecies existed but he knew it was not the time or place to comment. 'Yes ... you see, I repeat Miss Auphan's apologies for the suddenness of this ... the unexpected nature of our call and the purpose of it ... very sorry.'

'Sure,' Blanche Lecointe held fascinated eye contact with Yellich as she rapidly regained her composure.

'Well ... this is not easy to explain ... so I'll just say it, but in the first instance can I ask you how you know your sister is deceased?' He paused. 'What I mean to say is that even though your sister's death was registered, what identification was made of the deceased? Can you confirm the deceased in question was your sister?'

'Yes,' the woman replied softly, 'yes, I can.' She remained composed, impressively so, so thought all three of the officers. Given the unexpected nature of the call, the revealed purpose of it, Blanche Lecointe's speedy recovery of her composure was impressive. 'I identified the body in the Chapel of Rest. She lay in an open casket. I kissed her forehead. That is how I know it was Edith.'

The three officers exchanged eye contact and nodded slightly.

'That's good enough,' Yellich said. 'In fact it's more than good enough.' He then addressed Blanche Lecointe. 'It seems that a woman has been using your late sister's identity in the UK.'

Blanche Lecointe gasped.

'We are extremely anxious to find out the identity of the woman who stole your sister's identity. This lady had a North American accent, she knew this part of Canada and she had a Canadian passport in your sister's name ... your late sister's name ... and she herself was murdered a few days ago.'

'My...' Blanche Lecointe put up a hand to her mouth, 'oh, my.' She sank back against her chair. 'My...'

'We have good reason to believe the person who murdered her to be a Canadian, a Canadian male, and that he is now back here in Canada.'

Blanche Lecointe forced a smile. 'In Canada? It's still a lot of territory, largest country in the Commonwealth.'

'Appreciate that, it's an awful lot of pink on the map, twice the land area of the USA ... more ... in fact.'

'The big empty, but yes, it's a large country.'

'Again, all I can say is that I appreciate that but this is our only lead,' Yellich replied calmly.

'We have to start somewhere,' Marianne Auphan smiled, 'and this is the one address, the only address we have. There must be some connection between your sister and the woman who was murdered in England a few days ago.'

Yellich deftly plunged his hand into the large manila envelope he carried and extracted the passport found in Edith Lecointe's bedroom in her home in Dringhouses, York. He handed it to Blanche Lecointe, opened at the photograph page.

'That is not my sister, definitely not Edith. Not her ... no way, not even the slightest similarity, and before you ask, no I do not recognize the woman in the photograph ... what an evil-looking woman ... those eyes, heavens just look at those eyes. Edith had such warm eyes but this woman ... Who is she? Who is she?'

'If we find that out...' Yellich allowed his voice to fade.

'What can you tell us about your sister?' Ventnor asked.

'I'd rather you asked questions, it would be easier,' Blanche Lecointe smiled. 'I mean I could tell you a whole lot about Edith but none of it would be any help ... like how she took her coffee and all ... ask me of the details you need to know.'

'Point taken,' Ventnor smiled. 'You're right,

of course.'

'I can tell you that we were not full sisters in actuality, we were half-sisters. Same father, different mothers.' Blanche Lecointe leafed through the passport. 'She didn't go far, did she? The mystery woman I mean, just one stamp ... Heathrow. Where is that? London? Oh yes, it says so ... oh...'

'What is it?' Marianne Auphan sat up, suddenly alert. 'Have you noticed something, ma'am?'

'The date, the date the passport was issued.'

'What about it ... is it significant?'

'It is dated a year, a full year before my sister died.'

A silence descended on the room.

'Are you certain?' Marianne Auphan asked.

'Sure. Sure I am sure.' The woman's voice rose with impatience. 'It's easily verified, but yeah, I am sure.' She handed the passport back to Yellich. 'Go check. Go check. But I tell you that passport was issued one year, one full year before my sister Edith died.'

Yellich took the passport and checked the date of issue against the death certificate in respect of the passing of Edith Lecointe. He felt acutely embarrassed. 'Something we should have noticed,' he said. 'Elementary, but yes, the passport was issued twelve months prior to the death of Mrs Lecointe.'

'Miss Lecointe,' Blanche Lecointe corrected Yellich with clear indignation.

'Sorry,' Yellich smiled apologetically, 'Miss Lecointe. And it was issued fraudulently. The person who obtained the passport was not Edith Lecointe. Can you tell us about Miss Lecointe's death?' Yellich addressed Blanche Lecointe. 'I'm ... we are sorry if this is difficult for you.'

'It was recorded as being accidental,' Blanche, Lecointe replied softly. 'And it is not difficult, but thank you.'

'We'll have to take a fresh look now,' Marianne Auphan added. 'It is now raising suspicions.'

'Who issues passports in Canada? What is the procedure?' Yellich turned to Marianne Auphan.

'I believe it is the same system as in the UK, by post from the passport office. The nearest one to Barrie is Toronto ... completed form, a copy of the birth certificate plus two photographs, plus fee. The form has to be signed by a professional person authenticating that the applicant is who he or she claims to be and also that the photograph is authentic. I admit it's the damned easiest thing in the world to obtain a passport in somebody else's name and the passport officials, hard pressed as they are, won't be suspicious. Miss Lecointe's application won't ring any alarm bells about illegal immigrants, she is, after all, white European, mid forties, resident in a small city which has no appeal for ethnic minorities or illegals, nothing suspicious there at all. Her application will be rubber-stamped. Here, in this situation, Miss Lecointe was still alive when the passport was issued so there would be no death certificate to nullify the claim. But passport applications are not cross-referenced to death certificates anyway.'

'Not in the UK either,' Yellich spoke softly. 'Big hole in the procedural tightness methinks.'

'Indeed.' Marianne Auphan glanced at Blanche Lecointe and smiled. 'I am afraid we will be here for a little time.'

'Sure ... I'll fix us all some coffee.' She rose

from the table.

Moments later, when all four were sipping coffee sweetened and with milk according to taste, Yellich asked, 'So, could you tell us what you know about your half-sister? Did you grow up together? We need to go as far back as we can ... I am sorry.'

'No ... sure, it's OK, like I said ... don't be sorry for anything,' Blanche Lecointe smiled. 'Happy to help. So, well, I am older. I was planned; Edith was not planned and was fostered from birth. She was given our family name and then forgotten.' She shook her head, 'Horrible ... just horrible to do that to a child.'

'Where did she grow up? Do you know?' Yellich asked.

Ventnor remained silent, occasionally glancing at Marianne Auphan; less occasionally their eyes met.

'In foster care,' Blanche Lecointe sighed. 'All that unmet need ... Foster care can be like natural parenting, I guess it can be good or it can be bad. In her case, I don't know the details but it definitely wasn't good. Later I found out that she criminalized herself when she was still a juvenile and was sent to live with the nuns at a place called St Saviours. I don't know where that was ... or still is. Like I said, all that unmet need, poor girl. We had no contact at all with each other, then she suddenly showed up on my front stoop with a valise or two and said, "Hi, I'm your sister". Took the breath right from me. We even looked similar which was strange because girls are supposed to grow up to look like their mothers and boys like their father ... but me and Edith, we were our father's daughters all right. And that, let me tell you, was the first I knew that she existed.'

'You were not told about her?'

Blanche Lecointe shook her head. 'Not a word, not a whisper, not a hint. Nothing. But she had her birth certificate, on it were daddy's name and address and his occupation ... mechanic ... an auto mechanic. He was a blue collar, beer loving guy but I never figured him for a Lothario, always seemed to be a home boy, apart from Friday and Saturday nights in the Tavern but other evenings he was happy to sit home ... dug his garden at the weekends and took us on family vacations, so it came as a shock when Edith rang my doorbell with a couple of valises at her feet. Some shock.'

'She brought valises?' Marianne Auphan commented.

'Valises?' Ventnor queried.

'Suitcases,' Marianne Auphan explained quickly, glancing warmly at him.

'Yes,' Blanche Lecointe continued, 'that's the point, she wasn't visiting with her half-sister, she was looking for a cot and a roof, already.'

'And you let her in? I mean, you let her stay?'

'Yes, after we had chatted some and she showed me her birth certificate ... and we looked like each other and we fell to talking quickly. Yes, I had a spare room and she was kin, so no reason not to, but the agreement was that it would be for only a short while; she had to look elsewhere for something permanent. It worked out well, she stayed for little under a year, she worked and she paid fair rent, picked up after herself like a good house guest and did her share of the housework.'

'She took up employment?'

'Yes, she did. She worked in a realtor's in Barrie. She had office skills, you see. She had a good résumé and got a job quickly. It wasn't much, she was just a middle-aged secretary without a family, but she had a steady job and that was when the economy was beginning its downturn. I'm afraid I don't know what it's like in the UK right now but here in Canada ... well, there's not much work right now.'

'Same in the UK,' Yellich said. 'Myself and DC Ventnor here don't get paid much but we see life *and* we have security of employment. We are among the lucky ones and we are not ungrateful.'

'I know what you mean. I taught school. I have this house and an inflation-proof pension. I need to budget but I am also a lucky one.'

'Yes ... so you and your sister must have talked?'

'Yes, did we talk ... I mean did we talk ... we had a lot to talk about, a real lot to talk about, years to catch up on.'

'Did she indicate she felt to be in danger?' Yellich asked. 'Did she say that someone was out to harm her?'

'No,' Blanche Lecointe shook her head slowly, 'she didn't but you know, for all that we talked, and we had a lot to talk about, she was always a very guarded and a private person. She had a social life that I wasn't allowed to be part of.'

'Any friend in particular?'

'Sally Brompton. She was a co-worker at the realtor's. They would go out together two or three nights a week. I reckon Sally Brompton will be able to tell you more than I can about her private life. She worked for Andrew Neill Realtor...'

Ventnor scribbled the name in his notebook. 'We'll pay a call on her.'

'They're in Barrie near the terminal.'

'The terminal?' Ventnor queried.

'The bus terminal on Simcoe Street, very near your hotel,' Marianne Auphan explained. 'I'll let you have a street map, already, you'll need it.'

'Thanks.' Ventnor smiled briefly and held eye contact with her.

'So,' Yellich rested his arms on the tabletop, 'probably a bit of a difficult question, but what can you tell us about your half-sister's death?'

'No ... it's all right and essential that you know. She died of exposure one winter.'

Marianne Auphan groaned and put her hand to her forehead, 'One of those? It happens each winter, all across Canada ... it's so tragic ... cometh the spring, cometh the grief.'

'Yes,' Blanche Lecointe repeated, 'One of those. Her body was found near Bear Creek in Ardagh Bluffs...'

'It's quite close to here,' Marianne Auphan explained, 'and also quite a similar housing development mixed in with spruce plantations. You can seem to be well out in the boonies ... out in the country, yet you are just a short walk from someone's house or from a main road.'

'I see ... ironic though,' Yellich commented.

'Ironic?' Blanche Lecointe turned and glanced at him.

'Well, that was how the lady using your half-sister's identity died, of exposure in a cold spell, in an open area beside a canal ... not in woodland but ... nonetheless, she died of exposure.'

'I see what you mean, but Edith had no connection that I knew of with Ardagh Bluffs or with anyone living there.' Blanche Lecointe glanced out of her window. 'I well remember the last night I saw her, dressing up in her finery and she a middle-aged woman. She was going out on a date like an excited teenager. It was winter. Snow had fallen. More was forecast. She didn't come home. I filed a missing person's report forty-eight hours later, then ... nothing ... nothing ... nothing until the thaw, it was about this time of year when her body was found. It had lain under the snow all winter.'

'That is what I meant by "one of those",' Marianne Auphan explained to Yellich and Ventnor. 'Come each thaw ... come each spring ... all across Canada missing person's reports are closed. Sometimes there is evidence of foul play but mostly it is misadventure ... accidental ... very often young men walking home with too much drink inside them, they take a short cut through an area of woodland, succumb to the alcohol, lay down or collapse, snow covers their body and keeps it covered.'

'I see. Tragic,' Ventnor said.

'It's Canada ... and it's any country with heavy snowfall.'

'Dare say,' Yellich echoed. 'So can we please go back a little further if possible?

214

What do you know of her life before she turned up so unexpectedly at your door?'

'Not a great deal. She did talk a little about it, but not a lot. The foster home sounded more like an institution than a foster family. It seemed that it was a large house full of children supervised by a single foster mother. Then she was with the nuns ... she didn't talk about that at all ... and that says a lot.'

'I see ... and yes, it does.'

'It was out at Aldersea, the foster home, I mean.'

'That's an easy drive from Barrie,' Marianne Auphan turned to Yellich, 'by the side of Lake Simcoe.'

'Another lake?' Yellich replied.

'Same one really. Barrie is on Kempenfelt Bay but Kempenfelt is a bay of Lake Simcoe.'

'I see.'

'So...' Blanche Lecointe continued, 'Edith told me she left the nuns at sixteen years old so she must have been very vulnerable, no family ... no money. She moved to Toronto to live in the big city. I swear it never had any attraction for me. I always thought that Toronto is such a mess of a city ... not like

215

Montreal. I could live in Montreal. I really could live in that city. She returned to Barrie when she was in her thirties.'

'Did she marry?'

'No. Well, she never said she did ... Edith never had a ring on her finger ... and she used her maiden name. She had a warm personality all right. So neither of us are or ever were catwalk models but we were still not bad looking. She had a warm personality like I said, she was a very giving sort of girl. She had no career to pursue, just had office skills, which are good enough but hardly a substitute for a family. So you'd think she would be hungry for marriage, but no, she never did marry. Two spinster half-sisters we,' Blanche Lecointe smiled, 'that was us.'

'Where did she live before she turned up at your door?'

'Dunno,' Blanche Lecointe inclined her head, 'that will be one for Sally Brompton. I believe she could answer that question.'

Driving away from Blanche Lecointe's house along Wattie Road, Marianne Auphan said, 'It's looking like murder. I didn't want to say anything in there but it's a common

216

method of murder here, all over Canada really, pour alcohol down someone's throat ... or some other substance, carry them outside in a snowstorm, leave them somewhere, some semi-remote place ... and a stand of spruce at Ardagh Bluffs is ideal. Just perfect ... near at hand and not easily overlooked. Without a witness or a confession all the coroner can do is return a verdict of "death by misadventure" but in not a few cases we have our suspicions.'

'I'll bet,' Yellich replied from the front passenger seat. 'I'll bet you do.'

'Sometimes...' Auphan manoeuvred the car to avoid a pothole in the road surface.

'You're thinking of something?' Yellich turned to Marianne Auphan, as she straightened the course of the car.

'Yes, I am thinking of something and I am still angry, very angry about it. Last winter a sixteen-year-old girl went out dressed in a party dress, no top coat or hat, didn't get back home by the designated hour and her father refused to let her in, wanted to teach her a lesson about timekeeping, he told us, but it was subzero ... for all the clothing she was wearing she might as well have been naked...'

'Oh...' Yellich groaned.

'We don't know what happened to her, not exactly, and we probably never will, but in her desperation she most likely accepted a suspect lift from a stranger, anything to get out of the cold. Her body was found thirty miles away and so the next time her parents saw her she was on a slab. Some lesson about timekeeping. I wanted to prosecute but our top floor vetoed it. Dare say they were right. This girl was their only daughter, only child in fact. He might have been a bit of a hard father but in his own way he loved her very much. His grief and guilt were genuine and his wife left him over the incident. Just packed her bags and walked out on the same day they identified her body. No purpose to be served by prosecuting, so the top floor said. Now I think that the top floor was right but then ... back then I wanted to throw the book at him.'

'Understandable.'

'But here,' Marianne Auphan pointed behind her, indicating the Lecointe house, 'here someone wanted Edith out of the way so they could use her passport ... here is deep suspicion. We need to reopen the file on Edith Lecointe's death, already.'

Carmen Pharoah woke early. She lay in bed in her small but functional new build flat on Bootham and listened to the city slowly awakening around her, the milk float whirring in the street below her window, stopping and starting and accompanied by the 'all's well' sound of the rattle of milk bottles in metal crates, of the different, deeper whirr of the high revving diesel engines of the first buses, and the distant 'ee-aw' sound of a passenger train leaving York Station to go north to still dark Scotland, or south to London and the home counties where the day had already dawned.

She thought, as she lay under the freshly laundered quilt, of the other life she had once had, of the other life she had felt forced out of. She and her husband, both Afro-Caribbean, both overcoming prejudice by professionalism, observing the advice her father-in-law gave her and her husband upon their engagement, 'I am proud of both of you, very proud, but you're black, you've got to be ten times better just to be equal'.

And how they were ten times better! Both ten times better, both employed by the Metropolitan Police, she as a Detective Constable and he as a civilian employee, a Chartered Accountant, assisting in managing an annual budget of millions of pounds.

Then ... then ... what was it called? She turned and lay on her back looking up at the ceiling. 'Survivor guilt', that was it ... that is the phrase, 'survivor guilt'. Those who survive feel guilty for having survived. The awful news was broken gently by one of her senior colleagues. Her husband could not have known anything, he had said, death must have been instantaneous and the accident wasn't his fault ... not his fault at all, that they would be prosecuting the other motorist of course and then leaving her to face dreadful widowhood when she was still short of her thirtieth birthday.

Then she had, soon after the funeral, transferred to the north, to Yorkshire. She had chosen Yorkshire because it has a reputation of being cold and unforgiving in terms of its climate and landscape and its people are also, it is rumoured, hard and unforgiving; no one, it is said, can bear a grudge like a

Yorkshire man. An ideal place for a guilt-laden survivor to live until she feels the penalty she must pay has been paid.

In full.

'Got a hit.' Marianne Auphan leaned on the lightweight doorframe of the office which had been designated Yellich and Ventnor's office accommodation for the duration of their visit. She smiled a smug, self-satisfied smile and held up a sheet of paper. 'The prints of the deceased, that is your deceased, whose name is not Edith Lecointe, she is known to us.'

Yellich sat up and smiled, 'She is?'

'She is.' Marianne Auphan advanced into the cramped office which overlooked Highway 400. Ventnor also displayed a look of intrigue.

'Yes, the latents belong to a felon called Heather Ossetti. She has previous for minor offences but it's her all right, a regular felo-ness. She was convicted in Vancouver for shoplifting twenty years ago. Not known to the Barrie Police, not known to Ontario Province Police, so I went national.'

'Good for you,' Yellich smiled though not

fully understanding the Canadian system of data filing; city, province, national...

'Nothing violent though ... receiving stolen goods, non-payment of a fine ... she went to jail for that. So it's a strange pattern of previous convictions given that she is a murder suspect and not reading like the sort of person that someone would want to starve of food before murdering them. She's just a petty crook according to this profile.' Marianne Auphan sat in the one vacant chair in the office and as she did so she glanced out of the window at the towering grey clouds above Highway 400 and the houses glimpsed between the trees beyond the freeway. 'Snow in the sky,' she said, 'that's a snow sky.' She turned to Yellich. 'So how do you want to handle this?'

'Two pronged, I think.' Yellich turned from the window after studying a 'snow sky' of black mountainous clouds which seemed to be descending on the town on the bay. 'You'll be reopening the file in respect of the death of Edith Lecointe, I assume?'

'Yes, already activated. The file is being sent up from archives and I have talked it over with Aiden McLeer. He fully shares my

... our concerns and suspicions.'

'I see, well, it's your pigeon, you are the Barrie Police and as agreed, you have tactical command but if you'll permit, I would like to investigate the background of Edith Lecointe. She was not a criminal, is not a suspect so it would not be a criminal investigation as such. I can do that alone with your permission and approval. At some point she must have crossed paths with Heather Ossetti ... when I find that point I stop ... and consult your good self.'

'Agreed.'

'Perhaps you two could investigate Heather Ossetti? We both need to know who she is ... or was ... I mean that both the Barrie Police and the Vale of York Police need to know about her, so let's use one officer from each force and at some point our inquiries will converge.'

'Yes. Agreed.' Marianne Auphan and Ventnor nodded to each other and then looked at Yellich. 'Yes, that sounds neat and sensible.'

'I'll need a car,' Yellich said. 'Can you provide one for me, please?'

'No problem. We'll let you have one of our unmarked vehicles. Fuel up here when you need to do so. Do you want to fly solo?'

'Yes,' Yellich smiled. 'I'll squeal if I need help, but solo is preferable in the first instance. I'd be happier on my own on this one.'

Marianne Auphan took Ventnor to Hooters Bar on the shore of Kempenfelt Bay. Upon entering they were greeted by the Hooters girls in figure-hugging white vests and red shorts who cried out, 'Hi, welcome to Hooters' as they entered.

'I thought you might like it here,' Auphan smiled at Ventnor, who sat at a polished pine table by the window which overlooked the bay. 'It's very American ... in fact it is an American organization.' She sat opposite him and Ventnor noticed her large brown eyes dilate as she held eye contact with him. 'Just what a Limey needs,' she added with a soft smile, 'an injection of genuine North American culture.'

'Appreciated.' Ventnor looked around him. He saw that the bar was doing good business. It was perhaps, he thought, about half full and it was still early in the day. Large muscular men ate large portioned cheeseburgers and French fries and drank chilled beer served eagerly and efficiently by the Hooters girls. 'And if this is North American culture,' he said as a Hooters girl slid up to their table to take their order, 'then it's something that this Limey can get used to. I promise I wouldn't put up any kind of fight at all.'

'Good,' she smiled, 'so welcome to Barrie, Ontario province.'

Later, before returning to the police station, Auphan and Ventnor walked side by side along the shore of the bay, not talking, but occasionally their shoulders would rub gently.

Sally Brompton revealed herself to be a short woman, well presented in terms of her own dress sense, wearing 'office smart' clothing and large spectacles. She had a round face, close cropped hair. She had painted her fingernails in loud red paint and wore 'sensible' shoes, feminine but with a small heel. She talked with Yellich in one of the interview rooms in the realtor's office in which she worked. Yellich had been unsure exactly what a 'realtor' was and had been afraid to ask but from the photographs of properties for sale on the wall of the foyer of the building in which Ms Brompton worked he surmised that 'realtor' was Canadian for estate agent. It was in much the same way that he was disappointed to find that Canadians have 'tires', not 'tyres', but he was equally relieved to find that a lawyer is a barrister or a solicitor and not an 'attorney' and that a cheque is a cheque, not a 'check'.

'Oh my ... oh my,' she repeated as she sank further back into the yellow armchair, 'oh my.'

'Bit of a shock. I am sorry.' Yellich spoke softly.

'You could say so, though I haven't heard about her in a while. Losing her life in the snow ... it happens a lot in Canada ... but now you tell me there is more to it ... something sinister.'

'At this stage it is only a possibility.'

'We thought it was an accident but now you tell me someone stole her identity and went to England with it. What sort of theft is that?'

'Callous,' Yellich suggested. 'Perhaps callous is the word.'

'Yes, callous ... callous ... so callous. So, how can I help you?'

'By telling me all you can about Edith Lecointe, as you recall her, and anything she told you about herself. We have spoken to Blanche, her half-sister, but Blanche told us that Edith was a private person and told her little of herself.'

'Yes, she was very quiet like that.' Sally Brompton paused and looked to her left and out of the interview room window as a white single-decker Barrie Transit bus arrived at the small bus terminal and 'knelt' on its suspension to allow the egress and ingress of passengers with walking difficulties. 'We became friends when she arrived here to work. We were both of the same age ... we are ... we were lucky to have an employer who doesn't discriminate. I still am. If you are a clerical worker you have a distinct advantage in the job market if you are young and pretty. Most employers like an attractive typist or two to set their office off but Mr Neill, he seeks efficiency above anything else, so we got a position here. I think ... no, I know, Edith felt her lack of advancement in life more than I did. She had no family as you probably know ... no husband ... no children ... but I am fulfilled in that sense, soon to be a first time grandparent. So I don't mind a lowly old job but Edith, all she had was a lowly old job. She wanted more out of life than life had given her. But Edith, she got asked out by older men ... or men of her age but she seemed unable to settle, unable to commit. She was wounded, I think.'

'Wounded?'

'In here,' Sally Brompton tapped the side of her head, 'or maybe here,' she pointed to her chest. 'She wasn't insane, nothing like that, but just damaged emotionally. She had difficult years, a bad start in life.'

'Yes, she was fostered, was that a bad experience for her? Did she ever tell you about that?'

'Well, she didn't talk about it or about the time with the nuns and that's always a sign of something bad ... you must assume what you must assume.'

Yellich nodded. 'I know what you mean.'

'So that really was Edith's life, many dates with divorced or widowed men in their middle years. She wasn't a cougar though.'

'A cougar?'

228

Sally Brompton smiled. 'You'll have them in England but you'll know them by a different name. In Canada "cougars" are middle-aged women who seek younger men.'

'Oh yes,' Yellich smiled, 'sugar mummies.'

'There is a bar here in Barrie where a lot of that sort of thing goes on. The young men sit alone and the "cougars" approach and offer to buy the drinks ... all upside down ... all reversed ... back to front ... but Edith wasn't like that, her dates were of her generation, the sort of men that need to pop a little blue pill if they are going to satisfy their date.'

'I see,' Yellich smiled.

'But nothing for her ever got beyond one or two dates with the same man.'

'So there was no one special in her life when she disappeared?'

'No one, and I am sure I would know if there was. We went out socially from time to time as well as talked in here. I am sure I would have known if there was someone special, as would her sister in Midhurst, but you've seen her, you say.'

'Yes. Now the other question...' Yellich paused, 'the other question is, did she seem frightened at all?'

'Frightened?'

'Yes ... of someone ... of something?'

'Not that I recall but as you said and as I also said, she was a private person, she probably wouldn't have told me if she was frightened but I got no sense of her being in a state of fear ... but her emotional hunger took her to some worrying places.'

'Worrying places?'

'Dark bars on Dunlop Street.'

'Oh, our hotel is on that street, seems quiet.'

'Oh it is, during the day ... during the day it's a very quiet street ... but at night...'

'Ah...'

'The bars stay open until two a.m. and Edith would occasionally come to work with bloodshot eyes. It never seemed that it affected her work though; Mr Neill never had any complaints about her. She was very efficient, very good at her job. When we went out together we were always home early, but she went out alone occasionally.'

'Did she ever mention a woman called Ossetti ... Heather Ossetti?'

'Heather Ossetti? No, no she never mentioned that name to me.'

'I see. Where was the foster home in which she grew up?'

'Out on the coast at Safe Harbour, in Aldersea, by the side of Lake Simcoe.'

'Safe Harbour?'

'Yes, she said it was anything but safe and harbour-like, it was on a road ... called ... she mentioned it, an English name, an English place name famous in history ... where the Normans landed...'

'Hastings?'

'Yes,' Sally Brompton smiled, 'Hastings Road, Safe Harbour, Aldersea. Not a happy time for her.'

'Thank you,' Yellich stood. 'I'll pay a visit, see if anything is still there, or anybody.'

George Hennessey slowly and sensitively opened the door and smiled at Matilda Pakenham who sat propped up in the bed. He saw how extensively bruised about the face she was. Her body was covered in a hospital gown and the bed covers and Hennessey doubted that the bruising would be confined to her face and head. She forced a smile and said, 'Thank you for coming.'

'Well I did say you could phone me.'

Hennessey sat on the chair beside the bed and placed a box of chocolates on the bedside cabinet. 'Bad for the figure I know...' he tapped the chocolates, 'but I think you can make an exception under the circumstances.'

'Yes ... thank you ... I think I will enjoy them, and thank you again for coming, you were the only person I could think of to call. They put me in a private ward as you see ... well, it's not really a private ward ... it's a little room off the main ward. They exist because some patients need isolation ... what's the term? Barrier nursing ... if they have a contagion.'

'Yes, that's the term, "barrier nursing".'

'And the rooms are also useful so battered women like me don't get stared at by the other patients, so they shove us in here. I prefer it really. I am just not in the right frame of mind to spend the day chatting to other women.'

Hennessey thought the room was best described as 'cosy'. It had room for just the one single bed, and the cabinet and the visitor's chair. Windows on each wall above waist height ensured that it was well lit by natural light. A small radio with headphones was mounted on the wall behind Tilly Pakenham's head.

'So what happened?' Hennessey asked. 'I mean apart from the obvious. Perhaps I should ask, "how did it happen?"'

'I told you he was in the town...'

'Yes.'

'I told you that I sensed him being here in York. Was I right or was I right? So he found me last night ... he followed me home, followed me back to my little drum and jumped me just as I opened the door, pulled me back and shoved me into the alley beside the house ... but I scratched him good. I have never done that before but I have read about DNA so I knew what to do.'

'They scraped your nails?'

'Yes ... it was a bit uncomfortable.'

Hennessey nodded. 'Yes, it can hurt a bit but our officers are taught to be as gentle as possible ... we need the evidence.'

'I understand. Thank you again for coming.'

'My pleasure. So now he'll be arrested, we now have the evidence to put him away for this ... he won't like that at all.'

'Yes. This time I am going to stand up to him.'

'Good...' Hennessey smiled, 'good for you. So where now? I mean after you are discharged.'

'Nowhere.'

'Nowhere?'

'I mean I have nowhere else to go ... I want nowhere else to go. It's time for me to stop running.'

Hennessey smiled warmly at her. 'York is a good city to live in, although I always find it too small. I am a Londoner myself. You can't hide in York like you can hide in London; you can really lose yourself in the smoke.'

'Yes, I noticed your London accent. I'll settle here ... and no more of that.' She indicated her tin whistle which lay atop the bedside cabinet close to where Hennessey had placed the box of chocolates. 'I'll keep it though ... it'll remind me of the gutter.'

'What will you do? Do you have any plans?'

'Get educated. Just lying here or sitting here you cannot do anything else but plan. So I'll get an education.'

'Good for you.'

'I'll build on what I already have and I have quite a bit I'll have you know, George.'

'Oh?'

'Yes. I have university entrance level qualifications and I can operate a word processor. So I can work to pay my way if I have to.'

'And you ended up sitting in a doorway wrapped up against the cold playing a tin whistle?'

Matilda Pakenham closed her eyes. 'Yes.' She opened them again. 'Yes. Quite a fall from grace wouldn't you say? But it's a question of self worth. If you are battered often enough and told that you are no good often enough you come to believe it. After a while all you think that you are worth is a doorway and a tin whistle and a plastic coffee cup for folk to drop their kindness or their pity into. But it was you that began the turn round for me.'

'I did? I only met you once.'

'But what a once ... took me to lunch instead of dropping a coin into my plastic cup. I went straight home after that, and that night I combed my hair for the first time in many days ... I mean properly combed it. I even tidied up my little flat. So, thanks,

George, I really owe you one ... and you also gave me the confidence to stand up to him. I'll give evidence this time.' She paused and looked down at the bed sheets. 'I imagine you have a lady in your life?'

'Yes ... yes, I do.'

'She's very lucky.'

'I am very lucky. I know how fortunate I am.'

'You should marry her.'

'Perhaps ... one day ... but that's a joint decision.'

'Yes, don't I know it? So you'll arrest him?'

'We will. I won't ... our officers from the Female and Child Abuse Unit will do that.'

'I see,' again she paused and looked at the bed sheets, 'so, my future...?'

'Yes?'

'There's a university here, isn't there? In York I mean?'

'Yes, a very good one.'

'I'll apply there. I'll be a mature student, thirty-seven now, forty or forty-one before I get a degree, which I should have had at twenty or twenty-one, but I fell for the charms of Noel Sigsworth. Imagine swapping a classy sounding name like Pakenham to become Mrs Sigsworth ... what a silly sounding name, but I did it. We made such a handsome couple but I came back from my honeymoon with a bruise the size of a football on my back.'

'And you remained with him?'

'Yes, women do ... the apology, the promise it will never happen again ... the remorse ... the charm, and with that comes the feeling that it was somehow my fault all along.'

A silence descended. It was broken by Hennessey who said, 'Well, we'll arrest him and this is the first day in the rest of your life.'

Matilda Pakenham smiled. 'The first day in the rest of my life ... I like that, and you're right George, it starts fresh from here.' She bit her lip and looked thoughtful. 'George, can I ask you something and tell you something?'

'Yes, of course.'

'Have you ever come across a guy, and I mean a criminal, called Malpass? He and his wife, Mr and Mrs Malpass?'

'The name rings no bells ... criminal or otherwise. Why do you ask?'

'Because you didn't meet me when I was at

my worst ... I've been lower. I once had a bad drink problem.'

'Oh ... but quite understandable.'

'The reason I ask is that I met someone at the AA meeting and they invited me to join their private alcoholics club, meeting in cafes just to pass the time to keep each other off the booze. So I went one evening, the Malpasses were there, sort of like Lord and Lady among the alcohol lowlifers with no money. The Malpasses always paid for the coffee and nibbles to eat. They were suave, charming, just like hubby was suave and charming and so I was on my guard with them.'

'Yes...' Hennessey leaned forward slightly.

'So I went to their meetings a few times ... claimed to be dried out alcoholics but I don't think they were. They said, "Look at us, we've cleaned our act up, so can you."'

'I see.'

'But as I just said, I was suspicious because of my marriage. Anyway, one day they invited me to go with them for a day trip to the coast and when I declined they looked crestfallen ... I mean more than disappointed ... and also they looked angry. Maybe I am being paranoid or maybe it's women's intuition but I got the feeling that if I had accepted their offer of a trip to the coast I wouldn't have come back.'

'That is interesting,' Hennessey replied with a serious tone to his voice.

'I wouldn't have been missed. I was socially isolated and there was another woman who used to attend and suddenly didn't any more.'

'Oh?'

'And when I asked about her they said, 'Oh, don't worry about her, she'll have moved on ... it happens.'

'Malpass, you say?'

'Yes. Ronald and Sylvia Malpass.'

Thomson Ventnor glanced in an interested manner to his left and right as Marianne Auphan drove slowly along Scott Drive, Letitia Heights. He saw small detached houses built with brick up to a height of approximately two feet and thereafter the walls seemed to be made of aluminium sheeting, as were the roofs, and all painted a uniform dull green colour. Each house had a small porch in front of the front door and each porch seemed to him to have a white plastic chair upon it. Any car that was parked in the short driveway of the houses or at the kerb appeared to Ventnor to be elderly and of indifferent value. Again, he noticed that no one was seen in the area, no pedestrian upon the sidewalk, no one addressing garden or home maintenance for example. It seemed the norm to him that no one was ever seen in suburban Barrie, unless they were driving a car or were a bus passenger. 'Frost ... Kipling...' he observed.

'Yes, the streets round here are all named after poets, not throughout Letitia Heights, just this particular area.'

'I see.'

'Well, this is about as bad as Barrie gets,' Marianne Auphan turned to Ventnor and smiled.

'Listen, this is not bad at all, you should see parts of York, the places the tourists don't get to see.'

'Yeah, I'd like that,' she turned her head again to look at the road, 'that would be good.'

'Same in every town,' Ventnor observed dryly, 'always an underbelly.'

'Dare say. I have ancestors from near London, is that close to York?'

Ventnor smiled. 'Well, I dare say it's quite close if you're in Ontario but Londoners don't consider themselves close to York and vice versa. It's about two and a half to three hours by fast train.'

'Oh ... OK, but that's close, believe me, that's close. Here guys do that drive to work and then back again and think nothing of it. Kingston Female Penitentiary, which serves Ontario province, that's five hundred miles return from Barrie. I can do that journey in a single day.'

Ventnor gasped, 'That's not much short of the distance from the north coast of Scotland to the south coast of England ... astounding.'

'Different world, but we have freeways and drive cars that are built for distance working.' Marianne Auphan slowed the car to a halt outside a small house with an untidy garden, which was separated from the nearest house by a thick stand of spruce. It was similar to the nearby houses, with a brick built base and thereafter the outside wall and roof were the same sort of dull green painted aluminium sheeting. Marianne Auphan opened the car door and invited Ventnor to accompany her. They walked side by side and in close proximity up the short drive and on to the wooden porch which creaked under their combined weight as soon as they stepped on to it. 'You'd better let me do the talking.' Marianne Auphan pressed the electric door buzzer. 'The English accent could be a barrier, a lot of Irish descendants, a lot of French Canadians, they don't like the English, already.'

'Fair enough, whatever you say. Interesting though that you have English ancestry. Myself and Somerled Yellich thought you were French Canadian.'

'I am,' Marianne Auphan turned and smiled and looked at Ventnor with dilated pupils, 'in the main. You see my mother's relatives came over in the *Empress of Ireland*. They sailed from Liverpool in the early twentieth century and settled in Vancouver in the west of Canada but she married into a French Canadian family who lived here in Ontario and so I grew up in a large French Canadian family. Only my mother, and her relatives in faraway Vancouver, are my English Canadian connection, so, that's me, mainly French Canadian but with a little English Canadian in the mix.'

The lightweight wooden door was opened by a middle-aged woman with matted hair and hard, cold-looking eyes. Ventnor recognized the type, hostile, he sensed, very hostile towards the police. She held a cigarette in the corner of her mouth which she had smoked almost to the filter. She wore a tee shirt which hung loosely on her body and black shorts which revealed lower legs covered in hair. She was barefoot. 'Snow was called on the radio this morning so I expected that,' she spoke with a harsh rasping voice, 'but I didn't expect the police. You're going to throw me in the bucket. Again.'

'No need to show you our ID in that case.' But Marianne Auphan did so anyway. Ventnor did likewise. 'And no, we're not going to bucket you ... we do have plenty of room in there though. We're looking for information.'

'Just information?' The woman sounded relieved.

'That's all.'

'You'd better come in.' She stepped aside with unsteady and uncoordinated movements and the two officers entered her dark and musty smelling home. 'Sit if you want to but if I were you I'd stand, I truly would.' She indicated a pile of empty beer cans on the floor next to an ancient looking gas fire. 'All the chairs are damp if you know what I mean.'

'Yes, I can guess what you mean, 'Marianne Auphan replied, 'and thanks, but we'll take your advice and stand.'

'Sensible.' The woman sank heavily into an armchair which was ripped and torn in many places. She dogged the cigarette butt in an overflowing ashtray and lit another cigarette from a blue packet.

'Better for you to be indoors anyway,' Marianne Auphan spoke quietly, 'your feet look cold.'

'Can't really feel them,' the woman smiled, 'circulation problems.'

'You're not helping any by smoking and drinking already.'

'That's what the clinic told me but what else is there for me but smoke and the booze? I only got that for company.' She jabbed the air indicating an old television set in the corner of the room. 'And maybe that.' She indicated an equally ancient hi-fi system

244

which made Ventnor feel like he was back in Tang Hall YO10.

'So what do you want?' The woman lit the cigarette with an orange coloured disposable lighter, activating it with a clumsy twin-handed method. She inhaled deeply and breathed the smoke out through her nose. 'So what can I tell you? Hey, I thought I'd get snow but I got cops instead, but at least cops can talk ... snow don't say much.'

'We also listen. So are you Jordana Hoskins, already?'

'Yes.' The woman had the remnants of an Irish accent. Mainly she had a Canadian accent, thought Ventnor, but the Irish came unmistakably through. He fully understood the need to keep silent. His place was to listen, to look, to observe, and to receive an impression, but not to say a word.

'Yes, that's me, Jordana Hoskins, from Dublin City ... but that was forty years ago. I had no say in leaving; my parents brought me over on a boat. So it's the Garda in Ireland, and the police in Canada, all wanting information. So how can I help you?'

'Heather Ossetti.'

'What about her?' Jordana Hoskins was

clearly standing her ground against the officers. She wasn't denying knowing Heather
Ossetti but was also certainly very protective
of her. Ventnor realized that information
would not be easily forthcoming from the
woman.

'You and she were buddies, already,' Marianne Auphan said, 'what we call "criminal
associates".'

'Yes, we got thrown in the bucket together,
me and Heather. A few times.'

'We know. When you lived in Ottawa,
already.'

'Ottawa is a good province. I like Ottawa.'

'So where is she now? Do you know?'

'Heather?' Jordana Hoskins once again
drew heavily on the cigarette. 'Not seen her
for some time ... like years ... maybe a few
years.'

'You won't be seeing her again. Not in this
world anyway.'

Jordana Hoskins gasped, allowing a large
cloud of cigarette smoke to escape from her
mouth. 'She's dead?'

'Yes, already,' Marianne Auphan spoke
matter-of-factly. 'It happens to all of us,
sooner or later.'

'Yeah, I worked that out some time ago, but Heather...' The officers thought her reaction to be genuine, she definitely did not know where Heather Ossetti was.

'I'm afraid so. Don't like to bring bad news, not when we're looking for help, but that's the way of it sometimes ... like a hand in a glove ... bad news wrapped up inside a request for information.'

'Yeah, reckon it is.' Jordana Hoskins stared into the middle distance. Her eyes did not seem focused on anything. 'How? I mean Heather ... Can you tell me?'

'She was murdered.'

'I don't ever hear nothing about that.'

'In England. She was living in England when she was murdered already.'

'So that's why I haven't seen her, that's why I didn't even hear of her being iced. England ... you know I've never been there.'

'So, you and Heather?'

'Yes, just a couple of lowlifes, real losers ... skanks, thieves ... anything for a fast and easy buck, that was the Ossetti/Hoskins gang.'

'Being a skank isn't easy money.'

'Yeah, but you don't know that until you're in and once in, it's not so easy to get out and it becomes a way of life more than a job to do but eventually the younger women push you off the turf. That's what happened to me and Heather Ossetti. That's when we took to thieving ... then we got thrown in the can, had to happen eventually ... then we came to Ontario, looking for a new start. Heather comes from round here, so I came too. That's why we settled in Barrie ... Heather knew the town. Didn't do me any good because this is how I live. You see how I live. You see how I live, I'd be better off on a croft in Donegal. She was murdered in England?'

'Yes. The British Police believe a Canadian guy followed her there, tracked her down and did the business.'

'Jesus, Mary and Joseph.' Jordana Hoskins inhaled deeply and reached down beside her and pulled a can of beer from a pail of cold water which stood beside the chair. 'Fridge is out,' she explained. 'I'm on welfare, I can't afford to get it fixed or even buy another used one.' She heaved the ring pull off the top of the can with what Ventnor thought was a masculine grappling of her fingers. 'Not too early for the first beer of the day and a good reason to start.'

'That's one way of putting it, already,' Marianne Auphan replied. 'So who did she annoy ... do you have any idea? She rubbed someone up the wrong way.'

'Heather ... well...' Jordana Hoskins paused and looked down at the threadbare carpet at her feet.

'It won't have come from you.' Auphan read Hoskins's mind.

'I'll end up the same way as her if it does.'

'Understood. Mum's the word. She had stolen someone's ID when she died, she was running scared.'

'I just hear things ... some things I just hear. OK?'

'OK. So what did you just hear?'

'Well, Heather, she wasn't a real close buddy of mine. We did get into badness together but we were never close. Heather, she has, she had, an evil streak, you know. I mean well evil; she had the devil in her. I seen it once or twice and it, you know, it really frightened me. She was well angry about her start in life in a children's home near here ... but she had ... she was born with devil in her.'

'Which home?'

Jordana Hoskins drank the beer. 'On the coast of Lake Simcoe, can't be that many. If it's still there, those places open and close down again like stores that don't pay.'

'Did she ever mention a woman called Edith Lecointe? She'd be about Heather Ossetti's age, already.'

'And mine. Be...? Is she dead also?'

'Yes.'

'Jesus, Mary and Joseph.' Jordana Hoskins took another large drink from the can. 'Is there no end to it?'

'Edith Lecointe,' Marianne Auphan pressed, 'did she ever mention that name, already?'

'Not to me. Why?'

'It was her ID that Heather Ossetti stole. She was calling herself Edith Lecointe when she was murdered. And other names. She even had a passport in Edith Lecointe's name.'

'Did Heather kill her for it?'

'Don't know. Edith Lecointe was found frozen to death; her death was recorded as accidental.'

'She killed her for it.' Jordana Hoskins spoke matter-of-factly.

'She did?'

'Yeah. I saw it in her eyes most often but sometimes in what she did also. I can't say too much but that's got Heather Ossetti's fingerprints all over it. Get hold of their birth certificate, or a copy of it, any other useful documents and then kill them and you can take their ID. Simple. But clever in a way. Then you leave the area and go where nobody knows the person whose ID you have stolen. Moving to Toronto or Windsor would be good enough; you stay in Ontario that way ... but England ... England ... that is making sure, already. That really is making sure. She would not have gone to England unless she was frightened. Really well scared. Just look up the death of Nathan Fisco, three, four years back. Then you'll see what I mean about her fingerprints.'

'Nathan Fisco.' Marianne Auphan took her notebook from her handbag and scribbled the name on a blank page.

'Guy in his fifties.'

'About three years ago? In Barrie, already?'

'Yes. In Barrie.'

Hennessey stopped at his pigeonhole and

took the papers which had accumulated therein out and stood and read them. He found the usual circulars about office economy, requesting staff to write on both sides of a sheet of paper, use second-class postage and make all phone calls after two p.m. whenever possible. The papers also contained a reply from the National Police Computer in respect of his query about Malpass, Ronald and Sylvia. There was, it read, 'nothing known'. George Hennessey found that he trusted Matilda Pakenham's intuition, honed by her worldly experience of suave monsters, and growled, 'Not yet ... nothing known ... yet.'

Somerled Yellich strolled along the uneven brick sidewalk at the junction of Bayfield Street and Dunlop Street. This was, he found, the central or 'downtown' area of Barrie and was much smaller and quieter than he had envisaged it. An old hotel stood on the corner with a sign on the front of the 'V' shaped building dating it to 1876; it was three storeys with a flat roof, disproving, thought Yellich, the builders' maxim that 'flat roofs don't work' because this particular flat roof had clearly worked for nearly one and a half centuries. Further along Dunlop Street were similar flat roofed buildings which also appeared to date from the mid to late nineteenth century, behind which were late twentieth century apartment blocks that towered over the original buildings. To his right was the lake shore, a modern piece of metal sculpture, the 'spirit catcher', with components which swung in the breeze, and a cannon which sat forlornly on a piece of waste ground as if abandoned and forgotten by the army. Closer at hand a silver-haired woman had backed herself into the doorway of an unused building and stood talking to herself, youths placidly panhandled despite signs warning that it was an offence to do so. A white police car was parked carelessly outside the small police station in the bus terminal building with one front tyre up on the kerb and the other three tyres on the road surface. Yellich was particularly struck by the large number of morbidly obese people and also the large number of people who needed some form of walking aid, and all, he thought, too young, far, far too young to be one, or need the other.

★ ★ ★

Marianne Auphan drove Ventnor to Maple-view West. 'It's like the Pied Piper visited with Barrie one time already,' she calmly explained, 'played his flute through downtown and lured all the services out of the city to the suburbs. You want anything, you don't go downtown, you go into the suburbs ... bars, shopping malls, it's all in the suburbs and folk here work in Toronto for the main ... they don't need no downtown. I don't like the dead heart but hey, services in the suburbs are what folk want.'

'So I see.' Ventnor glanced at a complex of shops next to a Honda retailer.

'A few industrial complexes but not enough to support the city. Barrie's wealth is limited to Toronto or dependent on Toronto.' She pulled into a large car park and halted the car as close as she could to the entrance of a single storey modern looking bar called Dusty Jack's. Inside Dusty Jack's she walked up to the bar and sat on one of the high chairs. Ventnor sat next to her. A jovial young blonde in black tee shirt and slacks asked if she could help them.

'Two Buds.' Marianne Auphan ordered for

both of them.

The girl brought two bottles of Budweiser and two chilled glasses and placed them on beer mats on the highly polished wooden bar. Marianne Auphan said, 'Thanks,' and the girl smiled and revealed perfect glistening white teeth and said, 'You're welcome ... enjoy your beer.'

'I figured that woman was right,' Marianne Auphan forwent the chilled glass and drank straight from the bottle and did so deeply, taking large masculine draughts rather than small ladylike sips, 'it's not too early for the first beer. Unless you want to work some more, already?'

'Not particularly.' Ventnor also drank from the bottle.

'I got cut off here one time.' Marianne Auphan smiled at the memory.

'Cut off?'

'One of my girlfriends got herself out of a bad situation with a mad Irishman she was hooked up with, not married but they'd pooled their money to buy a house, so not easy to get out, but she did so. So then a bunch of us girls brought her here to celebrate, so we drank until we got cut off ...

wouldn't serve us any more … cut off and me a cop, already.'

'I see.' Ventnor glanced round the bar. Tables were set for meals with four places at each table. A few booths along the far wall were occupied by couples or two or three men. Four televisions were installed high up on the wall, all four tuned to the same channel which, at that moment, was showing a murderous fight between two huge ice hockey players, during a match, which rapidly escalated until all the players became involved in the brawl and the referee lost his balance and sprawled on his back on the ice.

'So,' Marianne Auphan put the beer down on the bar, 'we can stay here until the last dog is hung, or we can go to my place on Veterans Drive.'

'The last dog?'

'Until they stop serving, but that's not until two a.m. My apartment's just twenty minutes' slow drive away.' She sipped her beer. 'Well, it's what we've both been thinking since we met, isn't it?'

'Yes,' Thomson Ventnor replied in a shaking voice. 'It is what we've been thinking, already.'

* * *

George Hennessey found himself drifting off to a pleasant sleep when the noise jolted him into waking watchfulness. It had, he thought, been a pleasant evening. As was his normal practice, he had returned home to his house on Thirsk Road in Easingwold to be met by an excited Oscar. He had then taken a mug of steaming hot tea into the back garden and, whilst standing on the patio, sipping it, had told his late wife of his day, knowing that she was hearing him, listening to every word. Later he had eaten a simple but wholesome meal of pork chops and as his meal settled, had read a readable yet scholarly account of the Russian convoys during the Second World War. The author was, he found, able to evoke the freezing conditions and the mountainous seas and Hennessey learned that a near miss of a high explosive shell during the Second World War could still sink a ship by 'springing' its plates. Later, his meal settled, he had taken Oscar for his customary evening walk and had then walked alone into Easingwold for a pint of brown and mild, just one, before last orders were called. Later still he was about to succumb to a well-earned sleep when he heard the noise.

It was the sound of a motorbike being driven at speed along Thirsk Road, possibly, he believed, by a young man who thinks 'it' can't happen to him, or in these days of endless leisure possibly, Hennessey pondered, by a 'grey biker' who might see only frailty and senility ahead of him and so was careless of other road users, prepared to take the risk that 'it' might very well happen. In either case, the sound transported Hennessey back to the Greenwich of his boyhood when 'it' had happened to his elder brother. He recalled how Graham had lavished loving care on his silver Triumph, of how Graham would take him for a ride on Sunday mornings out from Greenwich, across the river at Tower Bridge, back across Westminster Bridge, round Blackheath Park and home. Then there was that horrible, horrible fateful night when he, abed, heard Graham kick his machine into life and listened as he drove away down Trafalgar Road, straining his ears to catch the last decibel of sound. Then there were the other sounds: ships on the river, the Irish drunk walking up Colomb Street, beneath his window, reciting his Hail Marys. Then, then ... that knock on the door, that distinct police officer's knock, tap, tap ... tap ... the hushed voices, followed by his mother's wail and his father coming to his room, fighting tears, to tell him that Graham had 'ridden to heaven', to 'save a place for us'.

Then there was the funeral. The first summer funeral of Hennessey's life and he saw how alien, how incongruous it was to conduct the ceremony of the hole and the stone when flowers are in full bloom and butterflies and bees are in the air; then there was the inadvertently insensitive playing of 'Greensleeves' from the ice-cream van, unseen, but close by. Two decades later he was to have the same feelings as he scattered his wife's ashes in the garden at the rear of his house, also on a summer's day. His father, by contrast, had had the fortunate good grace to die in the winter of the year and Hennessy thought it so fitting, so very fitting that the coffin was lowered into rock hard soil amid a snow flurry.

Hennessey had lived with the gap in his life where an elder brother should have been and always for him was the question, what manner of man would he have been? At the time he died, Graham had worried, if not alarmed, his parents by announcing his plan to leave his safe job at the bank and go to art college and there to specialize in photography so as to become a photographer. George Hennessey was certain that for his brother it would not be the sleazy world of the fashion photographer or the sniping world of the paparazzi but rather, for Graham, it would be the noble world of photo journalism, where a single image can alter a world opinion. He would have married, George Hennessey believed, successfully, he would have been a good father and a good uncle to his nephew Charles. He would have been a brother George Hennessey would have loved and would have been proud of ... all the might haves, and all the would haves, and all the could haves, and all the never will knows all taken from him because of a patch of oil on Trafalgar Road all those years ago. The thoughts ... the demons then, that night, kept whirring and whirling around Hennessey's mind, torturing him, until the beginning of the dawn chorus, when sleep mercifully rescued him.

FIVE

Monday, March thirtieth, 09.15 hours
*in which the story of Heather Ossetti is told,
Ventnor faces a decision and the culprit is appre-
hended.*

Park Gate Christian Retirement Community
was a new build development at the south-
east side of Barrie, close to the beginning of
flat, open country, a single track railway line
and local amenities, yet offered easy access
to the modest city centre should any resident
wish to travel in to downtown Barrie. At the
entrance was a tree, the trunk of which had
been carved with human-like faces evoking a
totem pole of native Canadian culture. Yellich parked his car in the small car park close
to the main entrance and reported to the
reception desk. He saw small shops, a hair-

dresser, a communal hall for meetings and church services, and a dining hall. All was clean and fresh and new and, he thought, it was also comfortable and homely. The warm mannered receptionist directed him to a tunnel from the main block to the residential block. 'Very useful in winter,' she explained, 'but convenient at any time.'

At the end of the tunnel – which was about two hundred feet long, Yellich guessed, and, intriguingly for a first time passenger, bent in the middle – he took the stairs up to the ground floor and then easily located the flat he sought. He pressed the doorbell. The door was opened by a tall, silver-haired woman who beamed her welcome, 'Mr Yellich, from England?'

'Yes, madam.' Yellich took off his hat.

'Reception buzzed me right now, letting me know you had arrived ... real good of them. Do come in. A visitor from England ... my...'

'Yes, I'm afraid so.' Yellich entered the small but neat and cosy flat with views towards the woodland at the rear of the complex. 'It's good of you to receive me at such short notice and so early.' He saw a small kitchen cum dining room, a sitting room, a toilet/shower and a bedroom. All an elderly person could want or need, and especially one within a self-contained supervised community of similarly aged persons. It was, he thought, not unlike a university hall of residence except for those at the other end of adulthood. He was well able to envisage similar complexes opening in the UK especially given Britain's ageing population. 'It's very good of you to see me,' he repeated.

'No worries, it gets me up and I am now free for the rest of the day.'

'Well, thanks, anyway.' Yellich smelled the scent of air freshener.

'Please, do take a seat. We seniors do so value visitors, even those on business. We see each other, and our relatives visit, but a new face is so welcome ... and from overseas. I take communal supper. I will have something to say at the table this evening.'

'Communal supper?'

'Yes, it's my choice. We can prepare all our meals if we wish or have all our meals in the dining room and anything in between. I don't eat much breakfast or lunch and so I prepare those meals in here in my little apartment but have booked in for the evening meal each day and that practise gets me out as well as keeping me in touch with the other seniors. Coffee? Tea?'

'Tea for me, please.'

'I ought to have known ... you English and your tea.' She smiled and went into her kitchen.

Moments later when Yellich and the lady upon whom he was calling each sat holding a cup of tea served in good china cups upon matching saucers, Yellich asked, 'Can I confirm that you are Rebecca James?'

'Yes, I am. Born to adversity James. That is I.'

'Adversity?'

'That's what the name Rebecca means, apparently. My lovely parents just didn't do their homework. But in fairness, I can't say it applied to me. I had my ups and downs like everybody else but I can't say my life has been one of endless adversity.'

'I am pleased for you.'

'You are married, aren't you, Mr Yellich?'

'I am?' Yellich was puzzled, but was enjoying the warmth in Rebecca James's eyes.

'Yes. You have that comforted look about

you ... married men have it, bachelors don't.'

'Astute of you,' Yellich inclined his head. 'Sorry it shows.'

'You can't hide it. Children, do you have any, can I ask?'

'One son. He has special needs.'

'I am sorry.'

'So were we at first, I have to be honest, but he gives us so much and a whole new world of special needs children and their parents has opened up to us and we have made some very good friends ... some really valuable friends.'

'Good, good for you and your family.'

'Thank you.'

'So how can I help the British Police?'

'I visited Safe Harbour this morning.'

'Ah...' Rebecca James smiled. 'My dreadful past is catching up with me.'

'Yes, but in a good way. Hastings Drive?'

'Yes ... yes, I lived there for many years. I was an approved foster parent. I have had many children through my hands, some stayed for many years, others were short term but I am proud of what I did. I know I was a good and a successful foster parent because some of the longer stay children visit me now here in Park Gate and intro-duce me to their children.'

'Well, my turn to say "good for you".'

'Thank you. I never had children of my own ... I couldn't ... medical reasons.'

'Sorry ... that must have been difficult to come to terms with.'

'Yes it was,' Rebecca James breathed deeply. 'So I settled for the next best thing, I cared for other people's children, but I did my best for all of them.'

'As you have shown by them visiting you. It is one of your children that I am calling in respect of.'

'Oh?'

'Yes, I dare say that I have some bad news for you I'm afraid.'

'They are in trouble with the British Police?' A note of alarm crept into Rebecca James's voice.

'No ... no, I am sorry but the child, now an adult, in question is deceased.'

'Oh,' Rebecca James put her hand up to her forehead. 'This has happened before. Parents whose children predecease them experience something they should not ex-perience but so many children have passed through my hands that occasionally I do hear of their passing. It is always a saddening experience. Always.'

'Yes, I can imagine.'

'A few did not make it through the danger years ... car crashes, bar fights ... often caused by alcohol and one or two girls died young, drug overdoses or abusive relationships which culminated in murder. So who are you interested in?'

'Heather Ossetti.'

Rebecca James groaned, 'Oh, yes, Miss Ossetti, yes I do recall her very well. She was not one of the good ones. You remember the good ones and you remember the bad ones. She was a bad one, a very bad one. Excuse me, I have her photograph.' Rebecca James rose from the chair with a suppleness and agility which both surprised and impressed Yellich and, as if reading his mind, she grinned and said, 'Yoga,' and added, 'not a recent convert either. I took it up when I was in my early thirties. Watch...' and, facing Yellich, she stood with her feet slightly apart, and keeping her legs straight, bent forward and touched her toes with evident ease and stood up again. 'Not bad for an old silver one, eh?'

Yellich gasped. 'I couldn't do that ... heavens ... not bad at all, very impressive in fact.'

'Yes, very few can do that once they reach adulthood. I love showing off to the doctors ... but, the album.' She left the living room and returned a few moments later with a large photograph album. She sat and opened the book which was bound in red leather-like material and began to leaf through it. Eventually she turned the book through a hundred and eighty degrees and handed it to Yellich. 'Girl on the left hand page,' she said as she did so. 'You see why I remember her as being one of the bad ones? Look at those eyes, is that or is that not the very essence of evil?'

'Oh yes...' Yellich gasped and slowly nodded his head. 'It chills me just to look at the photograph, but in real life ... how was she in actuality?'

'It's difficult if not impossible to hide the evil in one's eyes if it is there and at that age ... she's about ten years old ... she had still to learn the need to at least attempt to hide it...'

Yellich studied the photograph. He saw a

girl, smartly dressed, neat hair, she was smiling at the camera but not in a way that a young girl would normally smile at a camera in order to please, perhaps in order to comply with a request the photographer might have made, but the smile, Yellich thought, was more in the manner of the young Heather Ossetti sneering or laughing at the camera and the photographer, for above the smile were cold piercing eyes that just did not seem to be a part of said smile. The smile and the look across the eyes were separate, utterly unconnected with each other. 'Tell me about her,' he said softly, feeling chilled by what he saw.

'No. First I think I would like you to tell me what happened to her.'

'She was murdered.'

Rebecca James nodded. 'Yes, you know Heather is ... well, she would be the sort of person to invite such upon herself.'

Yellich told her the story.

'Running, with a stolen identity? That figures, her true personality just would not find a home anywhere, not for any length of time anyway. Well, perhaps only with a needy and a naïve man who had no insight, who

269

just could not see that look she displayed. So what can I tell you about her? Very little, I'm afraid, is the honest answer. I was only able to accommodate easily managed and biddable sort of children and that was not the manner of Heather Ossetti, not her manner at all. She was very disruptive, attention seeking, violent to other children but only to those weaker than her. She always attempted to befriend those she saw as stronger than her, but only to manipulate them.'

'I see.'

'A lot of damage was done to the building during the time that she was with me but I couldn't prove it was her.'

'Damage?'

'Initials carved in wooden panelling but not the initials H.O., initials of the other children who I knew would not do such damage. She very rapidly managed to turn all the other children against her and managed to create a very bad atmosphere. The children actually began to huddle in a group as if protecting themselves from her.'

'Interesting.'

'Frightening I would say, more than just interesting. As was the tendency of things to

270

disappear. That happened a lot when Heather was with me. Things would just disappear from the house and the children complained that their possessions had vanished. The possessions concerned were always small items that a ten-year-old girl could easily conceal and carry out of the house and throw in the lake, just to be spiteful ... but again, nothing was ever seen though I rapidly realized that Heather was responsible and that she needed a highly specialized care regime, and requested ... nay, insisted upon her removal from my home, and she left me a few days later. After she had been moved, no more damage was done, no single item or possession was ever noticed to be missing and the pleasant atmosphere returned.'

'What do you know of her background?'

'Very little again, very little information came with her. I believe she was given up for adoption at birth by her parents ... the files will be released to you upon production of a court order should you so wish. If I recall, she had a series of placements, none successful. Even her earliest placement in a nursery was difficult and the home she was in before she came to me was destroyed by fire and all the children had to be re-homed.'

'Arson?'

'Yes ... or fire-setting as it's known in Canada and the United States ... but the inquiry eventually focused on a deliberate attempt to start the fire by one of the children, but which one?' Rebecca James opened her palm.

'I think I can guess.'

'Yes, I think we both can. So she was with me for a few weeks. I didn't give in easily, as a matter of pride, but eventually I realized that not only could I not do anything for her, but she was a danger to the other children and to the building. It was a large, rambling wooden building, sealed against the rain by pitch as are many houses in Canada. Fire would have engulfed it very quickly and if she set one fire she could set another.'

'Yes, indeed. Where did she go when she left you?'

'St Saviours.'

'A convent?'

'Yes, a very strict order of nuns. Her situation was conferenced wherein it was deemed she needed that form of close supervision and tight control and that was the last I

heard of Heather Ossetti until you mentioned her name this morning. She did not come
to visit me, for which I am extremely grateful. Another of my girls went there also, a girl
called Edith Lecointe. She lost her life a few
years ago ... I read it ... died in the snow one
winter. Dare say they helped each other
through St Saviours.'

The recording light glowed red, the twin
cassettes spun slowly, silently.

'The place is interview room number three
at Micklegate Bar Police Station, York. The
time is nine fifteen hours on Monday the
thirtieth of March. I am Detective Sergeant
Fiona Rivers of the Vale of York Police Female and Child Abuse Unit. I am now going
to ask the other people in the room to identify themselves.'

'Detective Constable Tracy Banks of the
Vale of York Police Female and Child Abuse
Unit.'

'Rivers and Banks,' the man sneered, 'how
quaint.'

'Just your name, sir,' Rivers replied sternly.

'Sigsworth. Noel Sigsworth.'

'Detective Chief Inspector George Hennessey of the Vale of York Police at Micklegate Bar.'

'Alexander Milner of Milner, Rhodes and Ferrie, Solicitors, of St Leonard's Place, York.'

'Mr Sigsworth, you have been arrested and cautioned in connection with the assault on your ex-wife, Matilda Sigsworth, also known as Matilda or "Tilly" Pakenham.' Fiona Rivers delivered an ice cold introduction.

'Wife,' Sigsworth replied smugly. 'We are still married.'

'Very well, correction is noted, though you are estranged.'

'Is that the case,' Milner turned to Sigsworth, 'about being cautioned?'

'Yes. It was done by the book.' Sigsworth wore a dark suit with highly polished shoes and he reeked of aftershave.

'We will be charging you with Grievous Bodily Harm,' Rivers explained.

'A tiff ... nothing more.'

'A tiff which left her with six broken ribs and extensive facial bruising.'

'You have no proof and she won't press charges, she never does.'

'So this is a regular occurrence?'

Sigsworth shrugged. 'What marriage does not have its difficult periods?'

'This time is different,' Hennessey growled. 'This time she has made a complaint and we have your DNA. She managed to scratch you somewhere ... such as your hand...'

Sigsworth lifted up his left hand and glanced at the sticking plaster on the back of it. 'An accident,' he said.

'But it's your DNA ... from your blood, under her fingernails, that's all the proof we need.'

Sigsworth's smile was suddenly replaced by a cold hard glare and Hennessey saw the man who allegedly once said, 'I'm only nice to you if you buy something from me'. It was all Hennessey and the two FCAU officers needed to see. The case against Sigsworth was watertight although he could still charm a jury into returning a not guilty verdict. Such 'perverse judgements' are not unknown and men like Sigsworth are adept at jury manipulation. It was a chance the police would have to take.

'My job ... my career...' Sigsworth snarled. 'I'll kill the bitch ... she's dead...'

Hennessey glanced at the tapes turning silently in the recording machine and then looked at Sigsworth as the colour drained from the man's face.

'I didn't mean that,' he rapidly recovered his charm. 'You must know I would never really harm her.'

'But you said it,' Hennessey said. 'It's now a matter of record. We don't destroy these tapes.'

'So if some harm does befall Ms Pakenham,' DS Rivers added, 'we'll know who to look for, won't we?'

'And we'll be asking for an injunction to stop you going anywhere near her or making any form of contact with her whatsoever.' Hennessey advised in a soft, matter-of-fact manner.

Marianne Auphan stepped out of the shower wrapped in a black towel which Ventnor thought could be fairly described as being about the size of a small country. He propped himself up on his elbows in her bed as he watched her dress. Marianne Auphan occupied what Ventnor thought an ideal home for a single person. Rented, it had a built-in garage on the ground floor with an electronically operated roll-up door. From the garage a small door led into the utility area of the property where there was a gas heater, a washing/drying area, a downstairs toilet and plentiful storage space. Stairs covered with a fawn coloured fitted carpet led up to the front door of the property and turned again and led up to the living area on the first floor where there was a large kitchen, a dining area and a sitting area. The first floor was similarly carpeted and had pine furniture, within it a hi-fi system and also a sensibly sized television. It was, in addition, richly adorned with plants. Marianne Auphan, Ventnor decided, clearly enjoyed caring for living things. Above the living area was a bathroom/shower unit with a second toilet and two bedrooms. The property had an angled roof and access to the loft space was obtained from within a large walk-in cupboard off the larger of the two bedrooms. The rear of the property looked out across a 'deck' or elevated wooden patio to an area of open ground, then still snow covered, and industrial units about a quarter of a mile distant, the skyline being interrupted by a circular concrete water tower with the name 'Barrie' written large in blue upon a white background. The front of the property looked out across a car park to identical properties being part of the same development. Marianne Auphan's home could have been in the UK were it not for Canadian idiosyncrasies which Ventnor discovered with interest, such as the light switches which pushed upwards for 'on' rather than downwards as in Britain. The whistling kettle on the electric cooker he also thought particularly North American. For unlike the whistling kettles in the UK which make a shrill, high-pitched homely sound, similar to the whistles of British steam locomotives, when it boiled, Marianne Auphan's kettle made a low, mournful, soulful sound similar, in fact, to the whistles of American steam locomotives. He cared not at all for it.

'I'll drive you to the terminal,' she said, in a quiet but authoritative tone, combing her hair. 'Then you must take a bus in. I want to be discreet about this.'

'Agreed.' Ventnor levered himself out of bed.

'Take the thirteen bus out to Cundles East

278

and get off at Zehrs. It's a flat fare but you'll need the exact money in coins, already.'

Ventnor walked across the carpet to the shower.

'I don't eat breakfast, already,' she called after him, 'but if you want I can maybe do you an egg on toast ... or something quick like that?'

'No ... no...' Ventnor replied as the hot water drove into the sweat clogged pores of his flesh, 'whatever you do normally is good with me.'

Later, whilst waiting for the number thirteen bus at the Maple Avenue bus stop, Ventnor was amused to watch a group of young boys play soccer in blazing sunshine, dressed in tee shirt and shorts, in the road between two massive and stubborn snowdrifts, Canada in the spring. Later still he sat opposite Marianne Auphan as she pressed a mug of hot coffee into his hands and held up a manila folder. 'Nathan Fisco,' she said. 'Do you want to read it, or shall I give you the gist of it, already?'

'Oh ... the gist, please.' Ventnor sipped lovingly on the coffee.

'OK ... but listen, within these four walls

we're on the clock now, so we're cops … and nothing else … understood?'

'Clear as a bell, and agreed.'

'OK, good. So, Nathan Fisco, he died in a house fire about seven years ago.'

'Seven.'

'Yes, Jordana Hoskins was out by a few years but the drink does that to you, already.'

'I have noticed.'

'He died in a house fire, like I said.'

'Witnesses?'

'None. He was drunk according to the file, dropped a lighted cigarette on an alcohol soaked carpet and … woosh … but his lover at the time was…' Marianne Auphan let her voice fade to silence.

'Heather Ossetti … the fell Heather Ossetti.' Ventnor sipped his coffee.

'Yes,' she nodded, 'got it in one.'

'Hardly a difficult question.'

'So we'll pay a call on his nearest surviving relative. I have phoned him, he is expecting us.'

'OK, I'll finish this first, if you don't mind,' Ventnor held up his mug of coffee, 'can't function without it.'

★ ★ ★

The young woman knelt and picked up the book of matches. It had, she thought, an interesting cover. She resisted the impulse to throw it into the refuse bag. Given what her employer had told her about the recent police visit she wondered whether it might have some significance.

The man parked his small van on the concrete apron and once again, being irresistibly drawn to the location, he looked over the blue and white police tape at the small workshop. He once again thrilled to the isolation of the vicinity; he savoured the location as he once again felt the power surge. He thought it was wrong, what he had read about why rapists most often let their victims live, because you cannot have a power disparity with a corpse. 'Oh but you can', he said to himself as the wind tugged at his coat collar, 'you so, so can'.

Kenneth Fisco lived in what Ventnor thought was a modest home in North Barrie, wholly brick built of light shaded material with a darker grey tiled roof. A Humvee stood solidly in the driveway and, being a fawn colour, blended sensitively, thought Ventnor, with the house bricks and the colour of the bricks of neighbouring houses. Kenneth Fisco showed himself to be a slightly built, clean shaven, warm of manner individual. His handshake Ventnor found to be light but not overly so, not a 'wet lettuce' shake, and his eye contact seemed to be genuine. It was, he thought, as if Marianne Auphan was introducing one of her friends to another. 'Have you met Thomson? Thomson, this is Kenneth.' It was, Ventnor felt, that sort of meeting. The interior of the house revealed itself to be similar to the outside: neat and clean and well ordered. A photograph of the Queen hung on the wall of the entrance hall: no Roman Catholic French Canadian he.

'So, my father.' Fisco settled back into an armchair after both Marianne Auphan and Ventnor had, at his invitation, taken a seat on the settee. 'After all these years, finally there is some police interest. Has new evidence come to light?'

'Probably,' Marianne Auphan replied, 'but more in the manner of a possible connection with other ... other incidents. We have in fact become very interested in Heather Ossetti.'

'Oh,' Fisco groaned and looked upwards at the ceiling, 'that woman ... that ... female,' pronouncing 'female' with a great and clear and distinct anger.

'You didn't like her?'

'Oh ... it shows? No we didn't ... not me, or my brother ... or my sisters. She was such a deeply unpleasant and dangerous woman and we were children then, we couldn't defend ourselves and dad was always out of it with the drink.'

'She was violent?'

'More verbally than physically but we still had to learn how to duck.'

'What happened?' Marianne Auphan conducted the interview; Ventnor was content to remain silent.

'Well, dad was a good man but only so far as his lights shone and unfortunately for his children they didn't shine very far.'

'Really?'

'Yes, he was an adequate provider, can't fault him there, but he did take a good drink. He was also very needy, emotionally speaking ... I got that impression. I still have it really; I think that mother was a woman with five children, one of whom was her husband.'

'I have come across similar, already.' Marianne Auphan spoke with a low, knowledgeable tone. 'It happens ... or husbands with wives who are more akin to daughters ... very stressful and causes dysfunction in the family.'

'Yes, well mother died in a car wreck. She was a passenger, wholly the fault of the driver of the other car. After that dad lost the plot, really lost it, found it difficult to hold down a job ... really started drinking very heavily and began to bring all sorts of women home, one being Heather Ossetti ... but unlike the others she hung around, she stayed for months. For some reason our chaotic rundown old house was good enough for her to call home.'

'Hiding, do you think?'

Fisco paused. 'No, no I wouldn't say that. I think, looking back, that it was more in the manner of somebody taking the rough with the smooth.'

'Meaning?'

'Meaning she put up with our messy household because it was a meal ticket.

Father had a lot of money from mother's life insurance payout. When Heather left, he had nothing. He, stupid man that he was, that needy little boy inside him, had allowed her to be a co-signatory on his checking account. There were weekly withdrawals, all made out to cash. It was also our inheritance. I admit it would not have gone far between the four of us ... what would have been left when father died, but it would have been something. She kept him well supplied with booze until his account was empty and it was then that he died in a house fire.'

'What do you remember about the fire?'

'Nothing at all about the fire itself, we were not there. We returned to a burnt out shell. It's still there, the burnt timbers ... damn well planned though, the fire I mean.'

'Oh?' Ventnor sat forward. 'What do you mean?'

'You English?' Fisco asked, pleasantly.

'Yes. We're interested in Heather Ossetti also. So ... what do you mean by well planned?'

'It seems like it was, looking back, with the wonderful twenty-twenty nature of hindsight.'

'So what happened?'

'It was summer. She had bought a whole load of camping gear and she drove us to the coast.'

'The coast?' Marianne Auphan queried. 'From here?'

'Lake shore...' Fisco turned to her. 'I don't mean the ocean, I mean down by Lake Simcoe at Safe Harbour, near here. It had some significance for her I think but she never explained what it was. So she bought a heap of camping gear, ran us down to Safe Harbour at the shore of Lake Simcoe and left us to fend for ourselves. We were in no danger ... except from the mosquitoes, it being summer, but you learn to cope with them ... keep a smoky fire going, the flying tigers don't like smoke. There were other campers around and it was a lake so there were no tides to get caught out by. She said it was for our character development and our drunken old father just went along with it ... and we were children then. What we thought didn't matter. We really had no say in anything once Heather moved in.'

'How old were you?'

'That summer? Fifteen, fourteen, thirteen

and twelve. Mother worked hard, harder than my wife. We, my wife and I, we plan to space our children. But ... that summer ... each weekend was always the same; piled the gear and the kids into the back of the station wagon, down to Safe Harbour area on Friday and dropped us off. Towards the end she didn't even leave the car, just made sure we had everything we needed, that it was all out, and drove off. She'd collect us on the Sunday at about five p.m. Looking back, I now believe that she was getting us out of the way, not just once, on the weekend in question, but establishing a pattern. You see I reckon that she figured that if we kids were away only for the weekend when father died, it would look suspicious, but if we were away every weekend on a character building number then it wouldn't look so suspicious.'

'That's a good point,' Marianne Auphan said, 'it goes to premeditation ... very calculating.'

'That's what I think. But what was ... what is still very suspicious, really very suspicious, is that the old man only ever used to drink beer, just Budweiser out of cans or bottles ... non-flammable no matter how much he spilled, but on that weekend the carpet was soaked with whisky, so it turned out when the police and the fire service investigated. Then there were all the empty whisky bottles in the garage, they appeared from nowhere that weekend. They were not there when we went camping on the Friday but were there when we came back on the Sunday, giving the authorities the impression that father was a long term whisky drinker ... which, of course, is flammable.'

'I see,' Auphan nodded. 'You are correct, sir, that is very suspicious.'

'She hung around for a while after the fire, playing the grieving widow, even though they were not married. We had no home. After a while in a church shelter we were taken in by relatives, which was when Heather left us, and then we entered adulthood, inheriting nothing.'

'So what do you think happened?'

'She milked him for all she could, emptied his account ... that is certain ... but why she murdered him, why she didn't just leave him having taken all his money,' Fisco shook his head, 'that I will never know. That we will never know. Either he had woken up to the fact that Heather had bled him dry and was about to make things awkward for her ... or ... she saw an opportunity to do something she could get away with, even if that thing she saw was murder, just for the sake of doing it.' He shrugged. 'The house was fairly remote. It was already an inferno by the time the nearest neighbour called nine-one-one and by the time the fire department had arrived at the house it was a pile of ash. Then, like I said, after she hung around for a week or two Heather left ... once we were safely with relatives. She gave a statement about knowing nothing about how the fire started but overplayed dad's drinking. The coroner recorded death by misadventure. There was smoke in dad's throat you see ... I don't know the proper name.'

'Trachea,' offered Ventnor.

'Yes,' Fisco smiled, 'that's the word. Smoke deposits in his trachea, so he was alive when the fire was burning and he breathed in the smoke. That apparently made it accidental.'

'Apparently?'

'Well, I don't drink, I don't drink at all ... children of heavy drinking parents usually don't ... but I would have thought it would

have taken more than beer to knock someone out and so heavily that they wouldn't
wake up in a fire.'

'I would think the same,' Marianne
Auphan spoke softly.

'But no examination for poison in the
bloodstream was done and ironically, what
was left of him was cremated soon after. The
city finished the job the fire had started. But
the point is they then could not dig him up
and test for poison in his blood. The
Coroner just accepted that he was drinking
whisky and fell unconscious and dropped his
cigarette on the carpet and 'woosh', and
fortunately his children were at their usual
character building camp by the lake an
hour's drive away and Heather was in town
shopping. No one saw her leave the house, it
being remote you see.'

'Yes.'

'What else did you find out about her
private or her social life whilst she was living
with you ... anything at all?'

'Nothing. She had no friends that we knew
of; I believe that she used to spend her time
in McTeer's Bar on Dunlop Street ... if you
know it. You could ask in there. Been a long

time now but she might be remembered by someone ... she's the sort of woman who would make a lasting impression for all the wrong reasons. So it is highly likely that someone in McTeer's will remember her and may be able to provide some information.'

George Hennessey replaced the phone and stood and walked from his office down the CID corridor to the reception area. He stood beside the uniformed officer who indicated a young woman who sat on the highly polished hardwood bench on the opposite side of the room to the reception desk. Hennessey smiled at the woman. 'You wish to see me, madam?'

'Yes, sir.' The woman stood and approached the reception desk, nervously opening her handbag as she did so. She extracted a clear plastic bag of the type used by banks to contain coins. She placed the bag on the desk. Within the bag was a book of matches. 'Mrs Stand of the Broomfield Hotel asked me to drop this in, sir.' The woman had a timid way of speaking and seemed to Hennessey to be working very hard to avoid eye contact. 'I am to say that it has not been touched except by the chambermaid who picked it up, sir.'

'Thank you. Appreciate the care and consideration.' Hennessey picked up the bag and examined the book of matches. It read, 'Sign of the Whale, Barrie, Ontario'.

'It was found in the room occupied by the Canadian gentleman, sir. It had slipped down behind the bed and was missed during the first clean, sir. I am in York to buy bacon, sir.'

'Bacon?' Hennessey smiled.

'Yes, sir. It's cheaper in York.'

'I see.'

'So I am to hand it in to you when I am in York, buying the bacon, sir.'

'Oh ... now I understand. Well, thank you for this Miss...'

'Lloyd, sir.'

'Miss Lloyd, thank you, very much. Thank you very much indeed. And please thank Mrs Stand also.'

Hennessey immediately ordered an email to be sent to DS Yellich, care of the Barrie City Police, advising him that the Canadian he is seeking is probably a customer of the Sign of the Whale bar on Bayfield Street. He added that latents are to be lifted from a book of matches and will be sent to him.

That done he returned to his desk to complete the six month evaluation of DC Pharoah. He was enjoying writing it. It was a positive assessment, very positive. She was making no secret about her desire to return to London eventually, and he knew that when she did, she would leave a gap. A very noticeable gap indeed.

It was an old house, Yellich thought; at least it was old for Canada. Wholly built of timber, it had turret rooms and a porch on the upper floor as well as on the ground floor. It stood isolated from many nearby houses by approximately one hundred feet on either side. The rear garden rose in a gentle slope to a thick stand of woodland. The house was in a rundown condition and so badly in need of paint or varnish weatherproofing that Yellich doubted that it could be saved. Rot, he believed, must be, in fact could not have failed to be, well established in all that exposed wood. Two large Alsatians appeared at the front door window as Yellich closed the car door behind him. An elderly woman opened the front door but kept the screen door shut. She stared intently at him, unafraid and hostile. She was dressed in black and had long, silver hair. Yellich walked up to the screen door and showed his ID.

'That's not a police badge,' the woman snarled.

'You can phone the Barrie Police for confirmation.' Yellich spoke calmly.

'I have my dogs.'

'I can see.' Yellich looked at the two Alsatians who growled and barked menacingly at him.

'Well you look like a policeman, but the dogs will have your smart little ass if you try anything.'

'Understood.'

'So what do you want?'

'Heather Ossetti.'

The elderly woman groaned, 'That name ... that woman. So long ago now, thirty years ... more. How did you know she lived here?'

'St Saviours, they gave your home as her discharge address.'

'I see. They were a bit free with that information.'

'We assured them it was a murder inquiry

... so they relented. Your address was not freely given.'

'A mu ... again!'

'Again?'

The woman ordered the dogs to be quiet and then having opened the screen door led Yellich into a dimly lit, cluttered sitting room. The dogs followed and sat at the woman's feet, not once taking their eyes off Yellich.

'You don't seem to have a good memory of Heather Ossetti. It is Mrs Castle?'

'Yes. Mary Castle. Well, would you have a good memory of her if she killed your husband ... or in your case, if she killed your wife?'

'Tell me what happened.' Yellich sat back in the chair. The pattern was, he thought, becoming well established, and as such he anticipated hearing of a murder which doubtless had looked like an accident.

'She came here from the nuns. She was quiet, shy, reserved ... but that was an act.'

'You think so?'

'I think so. The report about her was good, positive ... a quiet girl it said, hard working, but those nuns don't stand any nonsense

295

and it rapidly became clear to me that Heather Ossetti had realized that she couldn't beat them and so she did the next best thing, she just didn't let the nuns at St Saviours get hold of her personality. You know the score; it was the old manipulation by obedience two step.'

'I see.'

'We were vetted by St Saviours. They don't like discharging their girls just like that, that's the quickest way to the red light district in Toronto.'

'Yes.'

'So they employ halfway houses, hopefully to give them some experience of family life. Both the girls we had before went on to get married but Heather ... she was certainly frightened of the nuns but not of us. Pretty soon she was testing the limits, then pushing them, never enough for us to order her out but enough for my husband to say we've made a mistake with this one. We could have turned her out ... she was seventeen ... could have and we damn well should have.'

'But you didn't.'

Mary Castle shook her head, sorrowfully. 'No, it was the onset of winter so we decided

to keep her until the spring. There is sometimes a false spring in Ontario, just when
you think summer has arrived, and it's then
that the snow returns with a vengeance.'

'Yes, it can be like that in the UK. So what
happened?'

'My husband died. Misadventure.'

'I am sorry.'

'Just out there,' she turned to her left, 'out
there at the rear of the house. Not out in the
backwoods among the spruce, but just a few
feet from safety.'

'Tragic ... that really is ... very tragic.'

'Yes. It makes it annoying as well as tragic.
So close to home. Hell, he *was* at home, just
outside the house and in his garden.'

'So what was the story?'

'It was the last of the winter. He went to
work as usual that morning ... and just didn't
come home, or so we thought. He worked in
Toronto and they still talk about the winter
of 1944 in that city when thirty-eight people
died in a snowstorm. It snowed hard that
day like the winter of '44. I was out that day
visiting my sister. He wasn't home when I
returned but I wasn't worried because Earl,
that was my husband's name, Earl Castle,

Earl always said, "If the weather is bad don't worry because I am a survivor. I'll be holed up some place, so don't worry." I assumed he'd stayed in his office overnight. He'd done that before along with his co-workers. So the next morning I phoned the company he worked for and was told his car was in the car park all right but that was because he and a co-worker, who also lived in Barrie, had decided to share a car home. They had made it home in a blizzard. The co-worker dropped Earl off at the front gate and had driven on home to his house.'

'He didn't wait to see him enter the house?'

'No, he couldn't see the front door from the road anyway ... near white-out ... but there is a guide rope from the gate to the door.'

'I noticed it.'

'Yes. So he, the co-worker, drove away. He also had to get home as soon as he could...'

'Yes ... understandable.'

'He said there was about two feet of snow when he drove away after dropping Earl off and it was still falling. The next morning the house was surrounded by snow, six to eight feet deep in places.'

'Good grief,' Yellich gasped.

'Well, that's Canada. The snow lay, and it lay, then eventually it thawed and Earl's body was exposed. Fully clothed, still holding his briefcase. For some reason he wandered round the back of the house and lay down.'

'What do you think happened?'

'I have only suspicion.'

'That's good enough. Between you and me, that's good enough.'

'Well, who was at the house that day but Ossetti.'

'She locked him out?'

'Don't think so. Earl was a strong, stocky man, he could have forced entry. He was also unlikely to go round the back of the house to force entry. If he couldn't get in the front he would have gone to our neighbours to seek shelter ... we are lifelong friends and they would have taken him in without a moment's hesitation. I came home later and got in without any bother. No ... I think something forced him or lured him out to the back of the house.'

'All right,' Yellich glanced uneasily at the

Alsatians.

'He had a slight graze on his forehead which could have been accidental, but also it could have been not so.'

'Yes.'

'The inquest was full of assumptions – there was no hard evidence to be had, just assumptions ... slipped in the snow, banged his head, became disorientated, wandered round the back of the house ... so it was recorded as being death by misadventure.'

'But your alternative theory?'

'Is that Heather Ossetti overheard us talking about her and that prompted a first strike, a pre-emptive strike. She banged Earl on the head but not sufficient to cause any severe injury and then led him in a semi-conscious state outside and let him lay down as the snow covered him ... and he succumbed to hypothermia and suffocation.'

'Not an unusual death in Canada I am led to believe.'

'Not at all and quite convenient if you want murder to look like an accident. Snow can be very useful in that way.'

'Did you notify the police?'

'Of course, the following day, but they had

their hands full rescuing stranded people, people whose lives were at risk. They couldn't leave that to search for a body in the snow and by that time, if he hadn't found shelter, that's what Earl would have been, a corpse covered in snow.'

'That could not have been easy for you.'

'It wasn't. We searched, me and her, the Ossetti female, we searched as best we could, poking the snow with long sticks, but as I said, it was eight feet deep in places. All I could do was wait for the thaw which came a few days later. It was the last snow of that winter and the true spring followed on not far behind. The snow melted so rapidly that there were floods and it was then that his body was exposed.'

'I am very sorry.'

'Twenty plus years ago now. I cherished his memory, I still do and that has kept me going as the years went by.'

'Heather Ossetti?'

'Stayed. She stayed with me. Couldn't be more helpful, eager to go shopping for me, which is quite a trek to the nearest store. Neither of us could drive and the bus service in those days was best described as indifferent. Then, one day, she wasn't here any more. She'd left a few possessions but had taken mine.'

'Yours?' Yellich gasped. 'Yours?'

'In my grief I didn't notice small but valuable items had gone missing ... jewellery ... Earl's collection of pocket watches ... the silverware. No wonder she was keen to go shopping, she was taking more out of the house than she was bringing home. So Earl had gone, our valuables had gone and she had gone ... like the snow ... just melted away leaving me alone in the springtime and the beginning of a very long autumn of my life. Just me. Earl and I had no children. So just me alone.'

McTeer's Bar on Dunlop Street was housed in what was clearly one of the original buildings of Barrie. It was of three storeys and flat roofed. The interior was darkened, the effect being obtained by tinted windows which Ventnor noticed could be wound upwards and thus spoke for the high temperatures experienced in the locality in the midsummer. Illumination on that day was gained by a few dim lights and numerous flickering television screens. Ventnor counted twenty-three and noted that each screen was tuned into a different channel from the others. The sound of the televisions was muted, the background entertainment being a radio channel which, as elsewhere when Ventnor had heard it, was playing songs which had been popular in the UK twenty years earlier. The proprietor was a heavy set, well built, bald headed man. 'Help you guys?' he asked, placing two meaty paws on the bar.

'Police.' Auphan showed the bartender her badge.

'I know,' the man smiled. 'I don't need to see your badge. It's written on your forehead. So, help you?'

Auphan levered herself on to a high chair in front of the bar. Ventnor stood. 'Ossetti,' Auphan said, 'Heather Ossetti.'

'What about her?'

'You know her?'

'She used to be one of the regulars. We haven't seen her in here for some time though ... like a few years.'

'You won't be seeing her again.'

'Oh, yeah?'

'Yeah ... she's dead, already.'

The bartender's head sagged. He allowed himself a generous few moments to recover. 'So what happened?'

'She was murdered. In England.' Ventnor spoke for the first time.

'You English, buddy?'

'Yes.'

'Another cop?'

'Yes.'

'So she was iced over in the UK?'

'Yes, that's a good way of putting it, a very appropriate way in fact.' Ventnor glanced round the bar. It was almost empty, just two other patrons sitting separately, both males, both reading tabloid newspapers.

'But you're over here looking for someone for it?'

'Yes.'

'Someone from Barrie went all the way to the UK to see to Ossetti?'

'We believe so. Do you know who would want to harm her?'

The man looked uncomfortable. He glanced around him. 'No,' he said, 'I don't know anyone who'd want to harm her.'

'Yes you do,' Auphan spoke coldly. 'Your body language is all wrong. We could come

304

back later when the bar is full. We could even take you into custody for withholding information … we have a lot of empty buckets waiting to be filled.'

'Won't make any difference, within two hours all the customers will know I've been talking to the law. Barrie is a very small town.'

'Just one name and we're out of here.'

'OK, but it didn't come from me.'

'Scout's honour, already.' Auphan remained stone faced.

'Tenby.'

'Tenby?'

'You should look into the death of Felicity Tenby. She was eight years old when she died … Ossetti's fingerprints were all over that incident.'

'Eight!' Ventnor groaned.

But by then the barman had pushed himself into a standing position and was walking away into the gloom.

'Tenby,' Yellich responded. 'Same name.'

'Yes.' Auphan sat at her desk.

Ventnor glanced out of the office window at the vehicles on Highway 400.

'Showed the barman at the Sign of the Whale bar the E-FIT and that is when he gave me the name Hank Tenby. He gave me his address as well but said Hank wouldn't hurt anybody.'

'That's for us to decide,' Auphan said, 'but we were given the same name, as we have told you. Same surname anyway.'

'So we visit,' Yellich addressed Marianne Auphan, 'but not all three.'

'Agreed. That would be too heavy handed. Just you and me, Somerled. Just you and me. The two lines of inquiry have now converged as we knew they would.'

It was, thought Yellich, a very accurate E-FIT. The man who opened the door of the condominium overlooking Kempenfelt Bay did indeed appear to be very similar to the E-FIT image compiled of the man who had stayed at the Broomhurst Hotel and who showed great interest in the old, cold, rambling house in which Heather Ossetti had recently once lived and worked. A little shorter than was described but the same man.

'You'll be the British police officer.' The

man spoke in a slow but warm voice. 'They phoned me, the people at the Sign of the Whale, telling me a British cop was looking for me and that they had given him my address.'

'Yes, I am DS Yellich, Vale of York Police.'

'Marianne Auphan, Barrie City Police.'

'How can I help you?'

'Be better if we talk inside.'

'OK.' The man stood aside, allowing the officers to enter his apartment.

Inside, the apartment showed itself to be on two levels, and built into a tower block. The rooftops of Barrie were seen below to the left and the right and the bay lay in front of it. The apartment was clean, neat and decorated in a modern manner, so thought Yellich, modern art prints on the wall, pine furniture and a flat screen television on the wall, the latter being, in Yellich's opinion, tastelessly large and more suited to a cinema than the living room of a home.

'You are Hank Tenby?' Yellich asked.

'Yes,' the man nodded. 'Please take a seat.' When he and the two officers were seated he said, 'This can only be about the Ossetti female.'

'Yes, it is. We are investigating her murder. A man of your description was seen apparently stalking her for quite some time before she died ... so you will appreciate our interest in you,' Yellich explained.

Tenby's reaction came as a surprise to both officers, for he sat back and smiled broadly. 'Well, how appropriate.'

'You, of course, know nothing about her murder, already?' Auphan spoke coldly.

'No, already,' Tenby continued to smile, 'but the news is very welcome.'

'It is?'

'Oh ... very welcome ... I can't tell you how welcome it is.'

'We've been asked to look into the death of Felicity Tenby. There is no record in our files. Who is she?'

'My niece, on my brother's side of the family.'

'What happened?'

'She died. She ate a laburnum seed.'

'Oh ... we have laburnum in the UK. It does happen occasionally that children eat the seed.'

'This was more sinister ... it was not an accident.'

'In what way?' Auphan pressed.

'My brother and his wife had hired the Ossetti woman as a home help during my sister-in-law's second pregnancy. They lived just outside Barrie, in Orillia.'

'Yes...' Auphan nodded.

'They had a house with a large garden. In the garden, tucked away among the shrubs right at the bottom, was a laburnum tree. None of us knew the tree was poisonous until it was too late.'

'I see.'

'Heather Ossetti was asked to watch Felicity for an hour or so while my brother and his wife went out to the mall. Came back to police cars and an ambulance outside their house. Felicity had swallowed a laburnum seed and had died.'

'I am sorry.'

'The family rallied round and Ossetti was there, full of tears, and she said in a whiny, pathetic voice, "I told her not to eat laburnum, I told her".'

Auphan groaned. 'You mean she put the suggestion into the little girl's head by telling her not to do it?'

'We believe so ... possibly, in fact highly

likely she said it in a very gentle voice and with a smile ... but none of us being there ... She might even have given her a laburnum seed to eat and said, "Try this, it's good", and Felicity was the sort of girl who'd eat one if an adult told her it was good.

'The women of our family saw through Ossetti before the men did ... all that female intuition ... but by then she had fled, she'd done what she intended to do, taken a life without being able to be prosecuted for it. But my sister-in-law is one of five sisters, they would have killed her for doing that to Felicity, and Ossetti knew that so she fled.'

'You followed her to England. Why?'

'To kill her,' he spoke matter-of-factly. 'I went to England to kill her. With me though it was more in cold anger than in hot passion. All I had to go on in terms of her whereabouts was a postcard she had sent to her buddies care of McTeer's Bar, a postcard of the city of York. I teach ... at the university in Toronto ... Modern History. I don't have academic permanency, just a series of short-term contracts, so when I had time I flew over a few times and gradually hunted her down. It took a year or two. Had to make sure it was her, she was well disguised.'

'We know.'

'Eventually I cornered her in the street in York with folk all around us. I told her. I said, "I have come all this way to kill you and you know what? When it comes to it you're just not worth it. I don't see why our family should lose two people because of you. We lost Felicity ... I don't want our family to lose me as well." I mean, twenty years in a British prison, then extradited back to ... back to nothing ... stripped of my job prospects, and too old to work anyway. She would have won twice over but I said to her, "Don't ever return to Ontario because if you do, then I know a bunch of women who will tear you apart" and since Ontario province is her home, that would leave her rootless for life. Then I turned and walked away ... went to London and the following day I threw a couple of coins in a fountain and then took the subway out to the airport and flew home.'

'We'll have to take a statement,' Yellich said, 'but that won't be the end of it.'

'I appreciate that,' Tenby smiled. 'My denial is not proof of my innocence. I will

311

cooperate all I can, but I have delivered myself and my family from evil ... delivered us from evil ... real evil ... a weight is lifted from us.'

Marianne Auphan stood naked at the window of her bedroom and watched as a yellow tractor trailer entered the yard of the business premises a quarter of a mile away across the open field which still boasted remnants of snow despite the hot sun and clear blue sky. 'Well, one of us will have to relocate...'

'I know,' Ventnor, also naked, lay atop the bed and looked up at the ceiling. 'I know.'

'And it won't be me, I am too strongly rooted in Canada, this is my home. You have a decision to make.'

'I know that also.' Ventnor rolled on his side and looked at her. 'I know that ... don't I know that, already.'

Carmen Pharoah and Reginald Webster drove out to the derelict business park where Edith Hemmings/Heather Ossetti had been held captive prior to being strangled and left for dead beside the canal. They had photographs to take of the location to complete

312

their report. As they approached they saw a small figure in a raincoat and hat standing in front of the unit in which Ossetti had been kept hostage and as they drew nearer the figure was recognized to be that of Mr Stanley Hemmings. His small red van was parked close by.

The two officers left their vehicle and approached Hemmings. 'I am just trying to get some closure,' he explained in a shaky voice.

'How did you know she was held here?' Webster asked. 'Not just at this site, but in this very unit?'

'You told me.'

'No we didn't,' Carmen Pharoah spoke quietly, 'we kept this quiet. No one, only the police, knew that this was where your wife was kept before she was murdered.'

'I think you'd better come with us,' Webster added. 'Do we need handcuffs?'

'No,' Hemmings shook his head slowly. 'No, you don't need them.'

The middle-aged man and woman, clearly, to an observer, very comfortable in each other's company, sat beside the log fire in the pub. They wore walking boots and had placed their knapsacks on the floor at their feet.

'Her husband was her last victim in a sense,' the man said. 'Harmless sort, worked in a biscuit factory, and who brought evil into the house where he had grown up. Could no longer cope with her endless complaints that compared him to the other men she had had, constantly telling him that she was now demeaning herself being with him. Eventually, the worm turned...'

'What will he collect, do you think?'

'Life ... but he'll serve only about five years, probably less ... come out to nothing but the dole for the rest of his days. Well, dare say we got our man and the Canadians got their first female serial killer.'

'Second,' the woman smiled at him.

'Second?'

'Yes, you're forgetting Karla Homolka ... remember? Murdered three teenage girls, her together with her boyfriend, one of their victims being Homolka's own younger sister.'

'Ah, yes ... how could I forget her? So they got their second female serial killer.'

'That they know of.'

314

'Yes, that they know of,' the man nodded. 'Frightens me sometimes...'

'What does?' She laid her hand on his.

'What is going on out there that we don't know about, all the missing person reports that should be murder inquiries ... but just think ... all that travel and the expense of same and the felon was under our noses all the time.'

'Annoying,' said the woman. 'Must have been a good experience for DS Yellich and DC Ventnor though. I would have found it very interesting.'

'Don't know what they thought about it. Yellich seems happy to be back home with his family...' The man paused. 'Ventnor, he's returned as though he is incubating a tropical disease. He's listless and detached and has somehow acquired the annoying habit of adding the word "already" to the end of every sentence he speaks.'

'Oh, that could be irritating, already,' the woman smiled, 'but you know what's happened there?'

'No.'

'He's in love, already.'

The man groaned and then fell silent as a

cheery young woman approached them carrying a tray of steaming food. 'The steak and kidney pie?' she asked.

'That's me.' George Hennessey released his hand from the woman's gentle caress.

'And I'm the cottage pie,' said Louise D'Acre.

316